Puffin Books · Editor: Kaye Webb
PS359
The Battle of Wednesday Week

Nicholas and Charlotte Latymer had lived with
their mother in the croft at Kilmorah ever since
their father was killed twelve years before. It was on
the wild west-coast of Scotland, with no electricity
and no tap water, but it was the most perfect
place in the world.

They knew they ought to be pleased when their
mother married an American widower with four
children, but they weren't. They would still
have Kilmorah and their mother, of course, but they
faced the awfulness of sharing something very
precious and then finding that the sharing had turned
it into something different.

'They can't *make* us get together,' said Nicholas
darkly, and the Grahams in America were thinking
much the same – this was to be a second Revolution,
when they would set on the English and drive
them out.

Later they all met at Kilmorah. Sometimes there
was so much noise from eight people all talking at
once that it sounded like a party, but at other
times it was pretty sticky. And after one extra
frightful row their parents went off on holiday,
leaving the children to learn to live together.
For readers of eleven and over.

Barbara Willard

The Battle of
Wednesday Week

Illustrated by Douglas Hall

Penguin Books

Penguin Books Ltd, Harmondsworth,
Middlesex, England
Penguin Books Australia Ltd, Ringwood,
Victoria, Australia

First published by Constable 1963
Published in Puffin Books 1968
Copyright © Barbara Willard, 1963

Made and printed in Great Britain by
Richard Clay (The Chaucer Press) Ltd.
Bungay, Suffolk
Set in Linotype Georgian

Contents

1 An Announcement 7

2 A Day in London 23

3 The House Called High Mount 36

4 Kilmorah 51

5 Grahams and Latymers 67

6 Picnic 82

7 Crisis and Challenge 99

8 MacBogus of Glengarble 109

9 The Laird 126

10 One Step Forward, Two Steps Back 142

11 Murdo's Storm 157

12 The Clan 171

1 | An Announcement

Nicholas was on his way up the stairs to Mr Anderson's study when, through the landing window, he saw Charlotte racing across from the music block. He paused and watched her – partly because even someone as well known as a younger sister can still look quite new and strange from an unexpected viewpoint – partly because it seemed to him that she must have received the same summons as he had and was rushing to answer it. And if a brother and sister, pupils at the same school, are suddenly called to the headmaster's study – surely it must mean that their mother, the only parent they have between them, is somehow involved?

Nicholas heard himself take a deep breath. Instead of hurrying to get the suspense over, he waited for Charlotte. When she looked up the stairs and saw him standing there, he knew she was going through all the same anxieties, for she was pale and her eyes looked wild.

'What is it? What's happened? Is it Sarah?'

At once, Nicholas became calm and old.

'How should I know? We'd better go and find out. You've got odd socks on.'

She was wearing coloured knee socks, and sure enough though they were both blue, one was light and one was dark.

'Why didn't somebody tell me?'

'I've told you, haven't I?' As she passed him at the head of the stairs he gave her a friendly whack. 'Brace up. Come on. I'll hold your hand, if you like.'

'I can manage.'

By jeering at her, however amiably, he calmed his own fears.

And rightly. For as they were called into the study the first person they saw was their mother, sitting in the armchair by the window. She had just had her hair done. She was wearing a new dress. She looked in the best of health and spirits.

'Don't ask me now. I'll tell you at lunch.'

Mr Anderson had given Nicholas and Charlotte most unexpected leave. After Charlotte had changed her socks and after they had both of them brushed their straight fair hair, which in each case badly needed cutting, they climbed into the rather shabby shooting-brake, and drove with their mother to the village. The County Arms Hotel was used to visiting-parents and had a restaurant that was packed full at week-ends and school festivals. Mrs Brough, the landlord's wife, who personally looked after the restaurant, knew parents and staff and pupils all by name, and even their favourite dishes.

However, that day being a week-day in the middle of term, the restaurant was empty except for local businessmen.

'Come down this end, Mrs Latymer,' said Mrs Brough. 'There. Take the table in the window and you can feel nice and private. Don't often see you in the middle of the week, do we?'

'I know. I feel rather guilty at being here.' Sarah Latymer smiled at Mrs Brough, and then spread the smile to include her son and daughter. But by the time it reached them, there was something a little uneasy about it. 'I've got family matters to discuss – there was no other way of doing it. Mr Anderson let them cut their classes.'

'Listen to that! They don't know they're born at that school, if you ask me.' Mrs Brough shook her head and rolled up her eyes in friendly disapproval. 'Well – excuse me for saying it, Mrs Latymer – they do rather go their own ways, don't they?'

'Perhaps they only think they do.' Again Sarah smiled. She put her hand over Charlotte's and held it tightly and warmly. A little as though she needed support.

'We don't even think we do,' Charlotte assured Mrs Brough. She and Nicholas were accustomed to remarks of this sort. Clere Combe was a co-educational school, and encouraged its pupils to learn about their own best abilities. Charlotte and Nicholas had been at Clere Combe since they first started school and now they were fifteen and sixteen; they could not imagine being anywhere else and liking it.

When they had given their order and Mrs Brough

had gone away, Nicholas and Charlotte looked expectantly at their mother. But as though postponing yet again what she had come to tell them – and it must be important – she talked on and on about ordinary things. About the term and what was happening, and if Nicholas felt he would do well in his exams, and if Charlotte had got rid of the cold she had caught a week ago.

Respecting his mother's handling of the matter, Nicholas made no attempt to ask questions. He felt both curious and uneasy, and he knew that she was oddly nervous. He didn't want to badger her with questions. Charlotte was always the impulsive one – it was she who cried at last in a voice of exasperated curiosity –

'*Please! Tell us!*'

Sarah picked up her glass and her children saw to their astonishment that her hand was trembling. Was it bad news, then, that she had come to break to them? That seemed unlikely, for it did not match her general appearance. It was not like her to look so elegant, just for a school visit. She was a rather absent-minded person, absorbed in her painting, just as inclined as Charlotte to put on odd clothes – happier in the remoteness of Kilmorah than in London staying with her old school friend, Myra Martin. It was from London she had come today, specially to see them, specially to tell them some news which now she could not bring herself to speak of.

'I find this very difficult, my dears.'

A look of immense shock flashed on to Charlotte's face and she turned as pale as the tablecloth.

'Kilmorah! The cottage! Burnt down? Sold? Has something gone wrong – and we've got to sell Kilmorah?'

'No – *no*! I'd never sell the cottage at Kilmorah. You know that. As for burning it down – it's like a rock.'

As she spoke, they were all seeing Kilmorah in their minds – the small scattered village along the water, with their own croft, a cottage and a bit of land enclosed by a stone wall, close by the edge of the coast. The coast was the west coast of Scotland, wildly magnificent. The cottage at Kilmorah had no electric light, no tap water. The garden was so scoured by the sea winds that hardly anything would grow there. It had belonged to the Latymers for as long as Charlotte could remember, but Nicholas could just recall going there for the first time, to stay with Aunt Mag, immediately after their father was killed. That was nearly twelve years ago. He had been a war correspondent for a famous newspaper, and he had been killed while reporting tribal troubles in Africa . . .

Nicholas looked at his mother and frowned. Her shaking hand distressed him. Suddenly, with an odd lack of surprise, he half knew what she was going to tell them. He hated to think that it could make her nervous. What did she imagine they were likely to say? All they wanted, he told himself and meant it most sincerely, was what made her happy. For years she had struggled to keep them all going and they were as tightly in sympathy with one another as only the best of friends can be. Nicholas sometimes felt as old as his mother – this was one of the times – and sometimes he felt she was as young as he was. And Charlotte, he knew, felt much the same – though she had for her mother the added sympathy that exists between women. Of course they quarrelled sometimes – what family can avoid that? – but there had never been anything serious.

Nicholas was a person full of attitudes. He was always acting and pretending to be someone slightly different. But he was utterly himself as he smiled at his mother.

'Go on,' he said. 'Or shall I guess?'

'Oh Nick, dear . . .'

'I might, you know. Charlotte might, too.'

'Might I?' Charlotte frowned. She stared at her mother. She took in her charming summer dress, her hair so newly and beautifully done. And she saw more than this. She saw a kind of pleading happiness in her mother's eyes – as though she was only waiting for one word to be blissfully content, but was not certain that that word would come. And in a way she was right to feel this, as Charlotte knew with a stab of shame, a quick flare of jealousy that came as she realized what this mysterious news might be. 'Yes. Nick's right. I might guess.' With that the troubled moment was past and she began to feel an upsurge of excitement. 'Well – shall I guess? Shall I? If you won't tell us, somebody's got to!'

Then Nicholas said, teasing: 'Sarah. Out with it. *Who is he?*'

At that their mother put her hands over her eyes and for a horrid moment they were afraid she was going to burst into tears.

'Then I have guessed!' Charlotte cried. 'Haven't I? Are you going to be married?'

Speechless, Sarah nodded. Then quickly she took her hands from her eyes and grabbed at her son and daughter and assured them: 'Not if you hate the idea. I promise. I'll forget all about it, if you hate the idea.'

'Hate it!' Charlotte's last reserves were completely flattened by her mother's anxious cry. 'It's wonderful!

Now we can go off to school each term with clear consciences!'

'What on earth do you mean by that?' Sarah was laughing and half crying at the same time.

'We always felt such shysters – leaving you alone for weeks on end,' Nicholas explained, grinning. 'We needn't give you a thought in future.'

At this moment Mrs Brough appeared with a laden tray.

'The pie's just out the oven. It looks a good crust, though I says it. Cuts lovely . . .' Her voice trailed away and she looked from one to the other. 'Well – what's this, then? If ever I saw three dogs with two tails . . .'

'What *do* you think, Mrs Brough?'

'Charlotte – please . . .'

'Why! I want everyone to know. Don't you? Aren't you going to put it in *The Times*?'

'Listen to that,' said Mrs Brough, dropping two forks. 'I knew there was something. I said to Mr Brough – you should see Mrs Latymer, I said. She's looking a picture, and what the gentlemen are thinking about . . .'

'Now everyone's guessed!' cried Charlotte. 'Isn't it wonderful, Mrs Brough? We've got her off our hands! Sometimes we've quite despaired.'

By this time Sarah was looking so happy that it was Charlotte's turn to feel like crying. Suddenly she thought how lonely her mother must have been, looking after them without help for years and years. Charlotte could not even remember her father, but from his photograph she knew he would be glad about this news – he had had a fair laughing face, rather like Nicholas's only thinner, and there was not a line in it that was not a generous one.

13

Charlotte felt so emotional and confused that she was never certain just when Mrs Brough fetched Mr Brough and Mr Brough fetched a bottle of champagne and the cork shot excitingly to the ceiling.

'The wife and I would like to wish you every happiness, madam,' Mr Brough said, raising his shallow glass and waiting for them all to do the same.

'Every happiness and many years of it, and you must bring your good man here one day, please, Mrs Latymer dear,' said Mrs Brough.

Nicholas drank his champagne with an air of enormous sophistication – Charlotte could see he was thinking of himself as a young man about town – and it was tiresome that she sneezed herself and had to put her glass down quickly before she spilt the lot.

'What a wonderful day this is,' said Sarah, looking round gratefully. 'I shall never forget it. Never. Thank you – all of you.'

Particularly she looked then at Nicholas. He was peering into his glass in a concentrated fashion, as though he was holding a crystal that magically told him all the future. And instead of a sophisticated young man, he was suddenly much nearer a troubled schoolboy. One thing he needed no crystal to tell him – he was not much longer to be the man of the family. He had felt a solemn responsibility for his mother and sister ever since his tenth birthday, when Aunt Mag had taken him on one side and said: *When I'm gone, you'll have to take over.* He had always done as she suggested to the best of his ability. Now that would all come to an end.

'What's he like?' Charlotte asked.

They were sitting in the little garden behind the

hotel, drinking coffee after lunch. Mrs Brough had been so busy dancing attendance on them that this was really the first chance they had had for straight questions.

'I think he's nice,' said Sarah.

'How old?'

'Three years older than I am.'

'Very suitable,' said Nicholas.

'I'm glad you think so. I wouldn't like to give you an unsuitable stepfather.'

'You never would,' Charlotte replied. She gave a slightly uneasy smile. 'Stepfather. It sounds very odd.'

'He isn't at all odd, though,' Sarah promised. 'Robert is tall, and he has a nice voice. And he has a very good laugh.'

'Has he got hair?'

'Yes, Charlotte, he has. Isn't that fortunate?'

'It wouldn't matter if he was bald, darling – we wouldn't mind if you didn't.'

'He has thick, distinguished-looking iron-grey hair and a sort of brownish complexion.'

'We don't even know his surname!'

'Robert Alan Graham.'

'Graham?'

'*Graham!*'

'Don't you like the name?'

'You know very well we like all Scottish names except Campbell and Dalrymple. But Graham! How wondrous! Why that almost makes us Gaelic ourselves. Oh *think* what they'll say in Kilmorah when you turn up as Mistress Graham!'

'Yes – well ...' replied their mother vaguely, frowning.

'Does he sound like a Scot?'

'Well – no, Nicky. He doesn't.'

'That's a pity. Perhaps he looks like one, though.'

'I think he looks and sounds what he is. An American.'

Both Nicholas and Charlotte turned to their mother in blank astonishment. She returned them a slightly defiant look, and said: 'Well?'

'An American?'

'Why not?'

'I don't see why not. Except that – '

'Except that what?'

'Well, you're such an English sort of person.'

'I don't see what difference that makes.'

'No – of course it doesn't make any difference. Not really. It's just – well, it's a surprise, that's all. I just took it for granted he'd be English. Didn't you, Nick?'

'Yes. But I don't know why.' He sat looking rather thoughtfully at nothing in particular. But he knew his mother was looking at him anxiously again, so he said, nodding his head like an old man: 'On the whole, Sarah my dear, I think an American stepfather is a rather distinguished thing to have.'

'And my goodness, I've thought of something else,' Charlotte cried. 'Is he rich, by any chance?'

'Not rich, no. Comfortable, as Mrs Brough would say. Things will be easier. Though of course he has his own responsibilities.'

'Yes, of course. What is his job?'

'He's a lawyer. An attorney, as they call it over there. He doesn't practise any more – not in the courts, I mean. He's legal adviser to his brother's business. He's in Switzerland at this very moment, or he might be with me today. His brother's in steel of some sort.'

Nicholas whistled. 'You've certainly moved into new circles, Mamma. Sarah Latymer's an artist. I hope Sarah Graham will be, too.'

'Robert collects pictures in a modest way. That was how we met. He came into the Chesil Gallery during the autumn exhibition. Do you remember I sold that little water-colour of the shore at Kilmorah? Well – Robert bought it. Then he wrote to me ... Then it all started.'

Charlotte lay back in her garden chair. She was now looking pleased, almost smugly pleased.

'I think it's all wildly romantic. It makes a wonderful story. I can hardly wait to tell it.' And she brought out one of the family sayings they had inherited, with so much else, from Aunt Mag. 'You really are a clever old caution, my dear.'

Sitting there in the sunshine in the flowery garden, Charlotte felt a little maternal herself – almost as though she was giving her blessing to the marriage of a dearly loved daughter.

'Can we come to the wedding? When is it? We keep forgetting the important questions. Do you think we'd get time off for it, if we went on our knees?'

'Of course you must come if you will,' said Sarah warmly. 'Now – there's a lot of complicated timing of jobs for Robert. So we shall be married in London very quietly, the week after next. The worry is that he's not due back until the day before the wedding. I'm afraid you won't meet him until the actual ceremony. Is that all right?'

'Oh, of course.'

'I must say, I have no fault to find with my son and daughter.' Then she added: 'So far ... Aren't there any more questions?'

'I can't think of any, can you, Nicky? I feel I know him already. Is it all right to call him Robert? Otherwise it'll have to be a nickname – and if you think up nicknames they're always corny. They must just happen. We really couldn't call him *Father*. It would be too awful.'

'He wouldn't expect you to, Charlotte. Let's leave that to his own family.'

There was what Nicholas always called a *loud silence*. Sarah looked at her hands for a few seconds. Then she looked from Nicholas to Charlotte. Both faces had changed from excitement to a startled wariness.

'I didn't think he would have been married before,' said Charlotte at last.

'But why not?' asked Sarah gently. 'Did you think he would have waited all this time to meet me?'

'I suppose I did.'

'I didn't wait, you know – did I?'

'No, but then you . . . Oh, I don't know.'

'What happened to his – well, to Mrs Graham?' Nicholas asked.

'They were travelling abroad and there was an accident. It was on a mountain road. A friend was driving. He was showing off, Robert said, taking the bends too fast . . . That was five years ago.'

Charlotte was remembering that Sarah had said Robert was three years her senior. So he could have almost grown-up children. Or not. There was no way of finding out except by asking and Charlotte could not bring herself to it. There were really rather too many shocks mixed up with the exciting news. It made her feel there might be more to come. Across the little garden table she looked quickly at Nicholas and then away.

When Nicholas spoke it was in the rather flat voice he used for questions that might have unpleasant answers.

'Do you mean you'll have to go to America, then? To – well, to look after things?'

'If you went – we'd have to go!' Charlotte burst out. How often had she longed to visit America – but not like this! 'We'd have to leave Clere Combe. We'd hate that.'

'There's nothing of the sort to worry about. Now

don't go making difficulties that aren't there. His mother looks after the home. After we are married, Robert and I plan to have two weeks in Paris, and then I shall go to America with him, just for a trip. Then we shall come straight back and spend the summer holidays at Kilmorah.'

'Has he been to Scotland before?'

'No, he hasn't. And he's longing to. After all, it's his true country, in a way. Please don't worry. Don't worry about Kilmorah or Clere Combe or anything. But make no mistake,' their mother said very steadily, 'my first loyalty is to you two. If you don't want me to marry Robert Graham – I won't marry him. But if I do marry him – then I must consider him in all things. Do you understand?'

'Yes. Absolutely,' Nicholas said.

Charlotte nodded, thinking as she did so: They're not grown up – not if their grandmother looks after them.

'And of course you're to marry him,' Nicholas said firmly. He wished he could tell her that she had been a perfect mother to them and it was time she thought about herself. But you couldn't say a thing like that – it might just go into a letter, but anything else was unthinkable. 'Now look here, Sarah, I'm still the man of the family, and I say you're to marry Robert Graham, and let's have no more hivering and havering about it.' He rapped on the table. 'Charley! Say you agree with every word.'

'Yes,' said Charlotte. 'All right. I do. If you like him, we're sure to. I didn't really mean that about going to America, anyway. I should probably like it like mad.'

An hour later, Sarah kissed them both, waved to them as they stood at the school gates, then drove away.

'She's worried,' Nicholas said miserably. 'She looked much happier when she first arrived. We didn't say the right things.'

'We did say some of the right things. It was just that there were so many shocks.'

'You weren't awfully tactful.'

'I couldn't help it. It burst out. It was because he's got children, I suddenly saw us all living together, one glorious happy family. Gosh, I thought – I *can't*!'

'How many do you suppose there are? I didn't dare ask.'

'Nor me. It was pretty dumb of us – now we'll spend all our days worrying.'

'Perhaps there's just one,' Nicholas suggested. 'One girl of fifteen or so. Clever. Horribly clever. Much, much cleverer than you or me – which wouldn't be difficult, but this one's a sort of genius. A prodigy.'

'Played chess at the age of four – that sort?'

'Yes. But this one was three and a half.'

'Good at quizzes, too.'

'Oh yes – brilliant. Probably on TV.'

Charlotte began to giggle cheerfully. 'She sounds ghastly. What do you suppose she's called?'

'Elinor?'

'That's not bad, actually. Can't you think of something worse?'

'Eustacia? No – I know! I've got it! Morag. To go with Graham.'

'And I've thought of something else about her, Nicky.'

'What?' He was catching her mood, laughing in his usual way, silently, with his eyes full of tears. 'Go on – what else?'

Charlotte spluttered. 'She wears mock tartan!'

'Colours?'

'Pink on green.'

'Ah – MacBogus – '

'– of Glengarble . . .'

That finished them. Speechless and weeping with laughter, they staggered up the drive and parted with feeble waves of the hand, one to overdue music practice, the other to a rehearsal for the end-of-term play, already in full swing in the library.

2 | A Day in London

Going to London for the wedding meant losing another
day's work – which was bad for Nicholas who was faced
with exams in a few weeks' time. He was moderately
clever. If he could get a university place he would read
history. Kilmorah had done that for him. The passion
for the place which he and Charlotte had developed
while they were still quite young had made them read
everything they could lay hands upon about the Highlands, about Scotland as a whole and Scotland's history.
In the case of Nicholas, this had led on to a feeling for
history in general.

All the time they were away from Kilmorah,

Nicholas and Charlotte were counting the days until they would return – patiently, philosophically, not by any means disliking where they were for the time being – but straining towards that one spot as to the place in all the world they most loved. They had already decided that not only their children but their grandchildren, too, would have the same feeling for it. Charlotte at times upset this plan for the future by deciding that she would not marry, but would settle in at Kilmorah for ever, and become a wise woman, brewing simples – whatever they were – and knowing about animals and the weather, being consulted by the locals and developing a little handy second-sight. 'I might learn to charm warts,' she often said, 'and be a water diviner.' Aunt Mag had been like that – except for the wart-charming and the water divining – and it was because of her that the local people had accepted the Latymers, Sassenachs though they were. Aunt Mag had given Sarah and the children a home at Kilmorah, and she had left the cottage to them when she died.

The day of the wedding dawned, as Charlotte observed, clear and bright – but she could not decide what to wear. Was it going to be a hot day? Or was the brightness of the dawning a threat of grey skies later, even rain? She wanted to look her best – neither blue with cold, nor red with the heat. She could wear a light print dress to which she was particularly attached, or she could wear the summer suit Sarah had bought her last holidays. Charlotte liked the suit even better than the dress because it was more grown up – you could wear a dress like hers whether you were four, fourteen or forty, but the suit had an air about it. She decided.

'What on earth are you wearing that for?' Nicholas asked, when they met in the hall.

'What's wrong with it?'

'You'll be too hot.'

'I shall be exactly right. Look at the sky. It's going to get cloudy and cool.'

'The weather forecast says normal summer temperatures.'

'Well,' said Charlotte firmly, 'this is a normal summer suit.'

After her visit to Clere Combe, Sarah had written a very long letter to Nicholas and Charlotte. Once again she assured them that if the idea distressed them in any way at all, she would give up all thought of marrying Robert Graham. As it happened, the announcement of the forthcoming wedding had already appeared in print, so they answered by sending a telegram. It took them a long time to compose. In the end it consisted of just six words: *Congratulations. See you at the church.* They had felt as they dispatched it that they had made up for any uneasiness they had caused their mother when she came to tell them her news ...

They sat in opposite corners in the train on their way to London. A sensation of change lay upon them very heavily. They experienced a feeling of solemnity – almost, Charlotte thought, as if they were on their way to a funeral rather than a wedding.

'Goodness, I've thought of something!' Charlotte cried, just as the train came in to Waterloo. 'We must be mad. We haven't bought them a wedding present.'

Nicholas was as appalled as she was. It just showed how selfishly they had considered the wedding.

'What on earth shall we do?'

'Is there time to get to a shop?'

'About an hour. But I haven't got much money. You?'

Charlotte shook her head. She said gloomily – 'I bet MacBogus has sent something.'

'Well if it's a pop-up toaster it won't be a ha-porth of good at Kilmorah ... We'll have to say we couldn't decide what to get because we hadn't met Robert.'

'I don't like it,' said Charlotte.

When they were in London, the Latymers always stayed with Sarah's friend Myra Martin – very often she went away for winter sports and so they had the place to themselves in the Christmas holidays when the weather made the journey to Kilmorah difficult. Sarah was staying with Myra now, and the wedding would be from her flat in Chelsea.

As soon as they came out of the station into the street, Charlotte realized that the temperature was indeed a normal summer one, and at once she began to feel much too hot. Everyone else seemed to be wearing light dresses, a fact which Nicholas did not hesitate to point out. Charlotte grew sticky with sheer anxiety and the conviction that she looked foolish.

It turned out that there was a little more than an hour before they were due at the flat, so they decided to look in a few shop windows – just in case they saw what looked like a suitable wedding present. They got a bus to Sloane Square. After a bit, without actually planning it, they found themselves outside the store where their mother had an account.

'What idiots we are,' said Charlotte. 'We'll get it here and have it put down.'

'On *her* account?'

'We'll collect the money somehow and pay it off before she gets back from America.'

Nicholas wanted so much to have a present for his mother that he gave in to this rather absurd idea.

Almost the first thing they saw inside the shop was a magnificent green velvet cushion with gold braid and tassels. It seemed to settle everything for Charlotte.

'That,' she decided.

'Let's just have a look in the china and glass department.'

They wandered among the glasses and tea services and casseroles.

'Charley – look! That would go wonderfully with the cushion.'

Nicholas had stopped before an array of Italian glass, the best piece of which was an enormous green goblet.

They stood arguing about this, deciding at last that they must take both the cushion and the goblet, in that way they would have a present apiece for Sarah and Robert. It took a little time to arrange the matter of the account. The two assistants, one for the goblet, one for the cushion, seemed uncertain about allowing them to take the things away. They suggested sending them.

'We simply must take them,' Charlotte urged, 'because they are wedding presents, and the wedding is today, and it's our mother's wedding – she's been a widow for twelve long lonely years.'

Nicholas said, as they left the shop: 'It was the long lonely years that did it. Full marks, Charley.'

He grinned at her over the top of his parcel, and she grinned back over hers, feeling pleased with herself and him.

It had been fairly cool in the shop, but outside the sun struck at them again. The parcels were beautifully packed but simply enormous. Charlotte could hardly get her arms round the cushion, and the goblet had been done up in a box padded with layers and layers of paper and shavings.

'We haven't got much time left now,' Nicholas said, glancing at the post office clock. 'Lordy, I didn't realize we'd been in there such ages. We'll have to get a taxi.'

They looked about hopefully. There was plenty of traffic and lots of taxis, but never one that was empty.

'We can't hang around any longer. Do you remember the short cut?'

'I should hope so – I've used it often enough.'

They set off briskly, Nicholas, who hoped he knew the way, in the lead, constantly changing the parcel from one arm to the other. Charlotte had to run to keep up with him. If she was not careful she would trip on some inconvenient kerb, for she could hardly see round the cushion parcel. Already she had cannoned into a perambulator wheeled by a coldly disapproving young mother.

Something went wrong with the short cut. It was ridiculous, when they had spent weeks and weeks in this neighbourhood, not to know every inch of the way. But there were several small roads that twisted or slanted unexpectedly, and after hurrying down one of these they found themselves travelling in quite the wrong direction. At ten minutes after the time they were due at the flat, they were still chasing about the back streets of Chelsea. Nicholas was growing increasingly pink and Charlotte's clothes were sticking to her. Her hair had flattened on her forehead and she kept blowing at it hopefully, for she had not a free hand to push it back.

The flat was in a mews and all the mews round about looked exactly the same. By the time they arrived at the right one, Myra Martin was on the corner looking for them.

'Where on earth have you been?'

'Buying wedding presents,' Charlotte panted.

'Your mother's frantic. She's convinced you're both lying somewhere in a mangled heap.'

'We only *feel* mangled. Where shall we put the parcels?'

'Oh heavens – rush inside with them. Hurry!'

Nicholas rushed, and rejoined the other two in a matter of seconds.

'Come along, for heaven's sake!' cried Miss Martin. 'The car's waiting – get in quickly. You really are a couple of idiots. Couldn't you have made an effort, just this day of all days?'

Although she sounded at the moment as though she could barely tolerate them, Miss Martin was really very fond of Nicholas and Charlotte. She had known them, as she always said, before they were born, and she sent better birthday and Christmas presents than anyone else they knew. She was looking so smart today that Charlotte felt more of a mess than ever. As they tore round the back streets once more, this time in Myra's dashing little car, she did her best to comb her hair – but Myra took the corners in such a fabulous fashion that the passengers had to cling on to prevent themselves being thrown from side to side. When they drew up at the church at last, Sarah was outside, looking wildly up and down the street, almost wringing her hands.

'Oh thank goodness! Are you all right? Darlings – what happened? Charlotte, you look so flushed . . .'

'They're perfectly well,' said Myra briskly. 'Sarah – compose yourself. Go inside. You're the bride – nothing can start without you. Poor Robert – he'll think he's marrying a mad woman.'

Sarah stood a moment longer looking helpless, then

she fled into the church. The others followed and took their places.

There were no guests but Charlotte and Nicholas and a business friend of Robert's who had acted as best man. His name was Stephen, and he was tall, be-spectacled and disinclined to talk. He made the fourth in Myra's car as they drove back when the wedding was over.

This was the moment when Nicholas and Charlotte would have been glad to remove themselves as quickly and quietly as possible. They would have given anything to escape the embarrassment of greeting their mother and wishing her happiness – and meeting for the first time the man she had chosen to be their stepfather. The presence of the silent stranger did not help, though Myra did her best by keeping up a flow of meaningless chatter to which nobody was expected to reply.

The journey from church to flat seemed half as long as it had done when they were driving twice as fast in the opposite direction. They turned into the mews and reached the door, which was standing open – and there was absolutely nothing for it but to go indoors and up the narrow stairs to the flat.

'Go on,' said Myra, giving first Charlotte and then Nicholas a sharp push through the door. 'Go and get it over. Take it from me – he's nice. You're going to like him.'

As Charlotte arrived on the threshold of the big living-room that was more than half the whole flat, Sarah and Robert Graham turned from the window and faced her. We shall never have her to ourselves again, Charlotte thought, in a doomed way. And for a paralys-ing second she felt as though she might make a scene. If

31

she were only no more than four or five years old, and could hurl herself on the floor in roaring tears and sobs of fury!

Instead, she felt her smile widen into a great grin. She rushed forward and threw her arms round Sarah and kissed her wildly, knocking her hat crooked and making her cry out.

'Darling! You'll knock me down!'

'You look *gorgeous*!' Charlotte cried – and knew she was shouting. She was hot again, red and untidy and looking like the last sort of girl any man would want to take on as a stepdaughter.

Nicholas, however, went to the other extreme. He was so poised he was positively bounderish, and Charlotte knew before he started it that he was going to turn on his eighteenth-century act that made him sound like a bad school play.

'Mrs Graham, ma'am – your most humble obedient. Your servant, ma'am, to obleege.'

'Oh Nicholas, do behave!' Sarah cried. 'Robert – they're showing off!'

Although she was laughing, they both heard the little ring of disappointment in her voice, and both knew that they were letting her down when they wanted so very much not to. There had surely never been such a tricky, difficult moment before for any one of them.

It was Robert Graham who saved the situation. He came forward holding out both hands.

'I am very deeply indebted to you two young people. You've had Sarah to yourselves for a long time. Thank you for agreeing to share her with me. I know it can't be easy.'

And although this was just the sort of remark they would call corny, with an American voice to make it sound in their ears like a film, the sincerity with which it was spoken gave it a guarantee. He meant what he said – and they knew he meant what he said. He was indeed thanking them. And by doing so he pulled them back to reality and made them themselves again.

'It must be awful for you, too,' Charlotte said.

Everyone roared with laughter – even Robert's silent American friend. To cover her confusion, Charlotte pounded on the immense parcel containing the green velvet cushion.

'Many happy returns – no, that's not right. Oh dear, I don't think I've ever been the bride's daughter before!'

She found herself looking up into Robert's laughing face. She laughed back – he looked such an easy, friendly person. And suddenly it was a party they could all enjoy.

The train was full when Nicholas and Charlotte returned to school. They had driven with Myra to the airport to see their mother – and stepfather – off on the flight to Paris. Then Myra had taken them back to London, given them an enormous meal in a restaurant, and finally pushed them on to their train.

'Thank you for everything!' they shouted, as the train began to move.

She shouted back: 'It was a near thing!'

And they knew all too well what she meant. Still, there had been no crisis after all, and rather to their surprise they found that they had quite enjoyed the day.

They had to stand for half the journey and when at last they got seats next to one another they seemed at first to have nothing to talk about. They sat, thinking their own thoughts, which anyway were much the same. Sarah – Robert – Paris; Sarah – Robert – America; Sarah, Robert – and Robert's family.

'Perhaps they're just as nice as he is,' Charlotte said, and she had no need to explain what she was talking about. 'Because he really is nice, Nicky.'

'Yes. Yes, he is. We ought to have known he would be. After all, Sarah chose him. As for his family . . . Well, that part seems pretty hellish, if you ask me.'

'I wish it was only MacBogus. I'd got used to that idea.'

'Well, it's four MacBoguses, my dear girl. So get used to that.'

'It's our own fault – we didn't ask . . .'

'Couldn't bear to know.'

'That's *why* it's our own fault.' Charlotte sighed and fidgeted. 'Even so – I can't think why they have to bring the whole lot back with them. Why not just two? Two at a time? We shan't have room to turn round at Kilmorah. Oh it's a mad idea! I don't see why, just because Sarah and Robert choose to get married, their children all have to get together in this way.'

'They can't make us get together,' Nicholas said darkly. 'If you want to know, I'm taking to the hills. It's guerrilla warfare for a start and a pitched battle when necessary.'

Charlotte was surprised. He was the reasonable one – it was she who made wild threats and extravagant promises.

'Perhaps it won't be as bad as we think –'

'It will be worse. Don't worry – you needn't join in my secret war if you don't want to.'

'A secret war . . . Oh Nicky, that doesn't sound right for Kilmorah. What in the world would Aunt Mag say?'

Nicholas said rudely: 'If you can't talk sense – then shut up. What's the use of dragging Aunt Mag into it? She can't help us this time.'

It had indeed been many years since Aunt Mag had been there to help them. Yet she had left behind her a collection of sayings and bits of wisdom that would never quite be forgotten by any of them who had known her. She had had a short way with quarrelling and fighting.

'There's only one good battle,' she used to say, 'and that's the battle of Wednesday week.'

Anyone could see with half an eye that this was a battle that never took place.

3 | The House Called High Mount

Lucy Graham stood in front of the looking-glass and combed her hair so fiercely that tears came into her eyes. A piece of stringy blue ribbon hung from her front teeth. She scooped up all her hair at last, dragging it back from her forehead, whipping the blue ribbon round it and tying it tight with a series of furious jerks. She might have been punishing her bitterest enemy. Once the ribbon was in place the grimness of her expression was more obvious. She clenched her teeth hard together even though they had now no ribbon to hold. There was something she must do that she would have liked to escape. The mail was in the box and it had to be collected. She, Lucy, would have to collect it. She always did. She liked doing it and the others left it to her. It was a privilege awarded to the youngest member of the family.

But today was different. She had been hanging out of the window when the mail man's car drew up. Mick Mulliner was driving, and as he leant out to stick the letters into the box he had spotted her and waved. He shouted something about the stamp. Then she knew that the letter they had all been waiting for had indeed arrived. Day after day they had looked for it. Now at last it was here. She must be a bit crazy, Lucy supposed – for she did not in the least want to know what was in the letter.

At last she turned away from the glass, slammed the door behind her and thudded down the stairs.

Alan was on the front porch, untangling a fishing line, being as usual exasperatingly patient.

'Hi, Lucy!'

'Hi,' she answered. But without any grace or warmth – angrily and flatly, her voice matching her expression.

'Mail's come,' said Alan.

'Sure, it's come.'

'You could've not known.'

'What else am I doing if I'm not going for it now?'

Alan said nothing more. He shifted his weight from one foot to the other, shrugging his skinny shoulders and settling again to the knots. He made Lucy mad, the way he would always be so patient and never snap out or anything, so you might almost think he was some grown, clever sort of man instead of a boy of twelve and therefore only three years older than she was. She swung past him down the steps and went with a loping stride, like an extra-large two-legged cat, to the mail box at the gate.

The box on its post was the only one in sight, for the Graham home stood at a twist in the road. The house was on rising ground. Southward, the Grahams looked down towards their neighbours' roofs, then away over those roofs, across the river to the mountains. There was still a good bit of land attached to the house, though no longer the acres that had once belonged. On the side of the hill to the north a crescent of woodland, white birch and maple, marked the present boundary. With the trees in high summer leaf there was no sign on this side of any other houses. But half-way through the fall they began to reappear, not too many of them, set about the hillside in a neighbourly but unintrusive fashion. Except for one ancient log cabin, all that was left of some early settler, the houses were all white-painted clapboard.

The Grahams' house had been there before any of them but the log cabin. The barn and the stable and the house itself were all under one L-shaped roof. There was a white painted flagpole on the lawn before the porch steps. The house was called High Mount. It was at Winterfield, Massachusetts, not too far from Boston. It was like thousands of other homesteads the length and breadth of New England. Except to the Grahams themselves, who accepted it as the best place in the United States and probably in the world.

There was a sale catalogue in the mail box, and the letter. Sure enough, it had a French stamp and there was no getting away from the fact that it was the one they had all been waiting for. For a moment Lucy had a wild longing to tear the letter up and go back into the house with only the circular.

Alan had stopped unpicking the fishing line and was staring down the path towards Lucy. He shouted at her:

'Is it?'

She nodded. She began to walk back to the house in a helpless way.

'Who for?' asked Alan.

'Granny. Who else? You know he always writes Granny for all of us.'

'Okay. So it's for Granny. Why don't you go and see she opens it? Don't you even care what he says?'

Lucy did not answer. She went through into the house, slamming the screen door behind her, so that Alan, who had turned to follow, sprang back shouting. She felt in an increasingly evil mood. There were certain people she would willingly have turned into toads, if she had known how. Not her immediate family, but some others she had only just learnt existed in the world at all.

Mrs Graham was on the back porch, and Nan was with her. Between them they were making a dress for Nan to wear at a barbecue in the village next Saturday, and the porch seemed to be full of cut pieces of candy-striped cotton in blue and white.

Her grandmother looked up over the sewing-machine as Lucy appeared, and Nan moved so sharply that she upset the pins.

'Now look!' she wailed.

'Oh there!' cried Mrs Graham, taking the letter that Lucy handed silently. 'It's your father! Now isn't that nice?' She looked from Lucy to Alan to Nan. 'Where's Roderick? Alan – call your brother in. I'm just longing to read this letter.'

'I guess he's in the woodshed with Satan,' Alan said. He went to the steps and yelled into the garden: 'Hi, Rod! C'mon in and leave that old snake alone. There's a letter from Daddy.'

'Why can't that boy make do with some civilized pet?' Mrs Graham cried, beginning to slit the envelope.

'Satan's not such a bad snake, Granny. Not like that mean old serpent he had last time.'

'He shouldn't have given it such a mean name, then. I wish he'd get interested in some nice dog.' Mrs Graham pulled the letter from its envelope and waved it, still folded. 'Now, I'm not going to open this till you're all here . . . There you are, Roderick. Come along in. Your father's written.'

Roderick was almost the same as Alan, except that he was a year younger.

'What's he say?' Roderick asked. He folded his legs under him and sat on the ground; he was good at such things.

'We don't know till we read it, and we've been waiting for you. I guess he's writing to thank you for the presents, for a start. There's no man this side of the grave can resist a pair of gold cuff links. And I'm sure Sarah was every bit as happy with that lovely bracelet.'

Nan looked at Lucy, quickly and nervously. Nan was thin, like the rest of them, with soft dark brown hair and small pliable hands that were astonishingly strong and capable. But although Nan was sixteen and the eldest, Lucy, the youngest, was somehow the boss. She had been almost a baby when their mother was killed and they had all fussed over her and taken care of her. Lucy was no spoilt darling, but she was strong willed and unpredictable. It was not only Nan, at this particular moment, who flicked Lucy a wary glance. Even their grandmother looked at her in a challenging way, as though defying her to make the disagreeable or crabby remark that might upset them all.

Lucy indeed bit back half a dozen such remarks, of

which the least offensive was *Oh her,* and remained stolidly silent.

So Mrs Graham unfolded the letter and began to read.

'Sarah and I were married yesterday,' Robert had written from Paris. 'It was a very quiet affair, in a little old church near where she stays in London. I wish you could have been there, but that was a little too tricky to fix up. But we have a plan we think you are going to like. We leave Paris the end of next week and then set out for the U.S.A. Sarah wants to meet my family with as little delay as she can. I believe she is afraid you may not be pleased at your old man marrying again – but I tell her you've each got as good taste as I have, so there's no doubt about how well we'll all get along together . . .'

'I don't see that. I don't see how he can be so sure.'

'Lucy! Be quiet and let me finish reading.' Mrs Graham repeated the line she had read, very firmly indeed: 'So there's no doubt about how well we'll all get along together. The plan is, we shall stay at High Mount for a while, but as soon as the summer vacation starts what do you say we all fly the Atlantic together –'

This time it was Roderick who broke out: 'Go to England? Is that what he means? It sure is, Granny! He knows we've got things to do here –'.

'– fly the Atlantic together,' repeated his grandmother, 'to spend six weeks or so at Sarah's cottage. It's on the West Coast of Scotland, at Kilmorah in Argyllshire.'

All the time the letter was being read, Nan had been on the floor, picking up her spilt pins with a magnet. Now she looked up for the first time.

'Scotland!'

'That's what it says, Nan. *Kilmorah, in Argyllshire, way down the Sound of Mull . . .*'

'Oh, glory be,' said Nan, sitting back on her heels and shutting her eyes tight. 'That can't be so far from Appin. Ardtornish is in Argyll. Kilmorah! What a name! What do you think, Granny? Could you expect to see Skye from there? The Cuillins?'

'You all of you know more about the map of Scotland than I ever did. I'm only a Graham by marriage, my girl. I never went to Scotland and maybe I never will. And I never felt the pull of it, the way the Grahams do.'

The pull of it. That was a good way to describe it, Lucy thought. Nan thought so, too. She sat there on her heels, looking down at the magnet and the pins, as though the magnet were Scotland and the pins were the Grahams. They none of them quite knew when *the pull of it* began, or how it started. Of course they had caught the idea from their father, who had heard his own grandfather tell tales of what was still home to him. They had read Stevenson and Scott as a matter of course, and learnt Scots songs and read the legends of the country. They knew about clans and tartans and the battle honours of the Scottish regiments . . . Even so, just when the whole business had become such a passion with them that it was like speaking a second language, they were never likely to decide. And now, without warning, their father confronted them with the certainty of a trip to the place of all others they had yearned after and dreamt about.

Inside herself, Lucy groaned. If she had been offered a trip to Scotland at any other time, through any other cause, she would have been delirious with joy. Now she did not know what to think. She had made up her mind about Sarah Latymer – only she was Sarah Graham now – and she had no wish to change her views. Why had no one told her that Sarah lived in Scotland – then she might have reserved judgement until they met? There were times, Lucy discovered, when good coming out of evil could be highly disconcerting.

Nan was smiling in a wavering, incredulous fashion. She was clearly no good as an ally, and Lucy dismissed her. She looked wildly at the boys, but it was obvious that a thaw had set in there, too. They had been scowling – now they were grinning. Alan gave Roderick a great dig in the ribs, and Roderick cried 'Hoots, mon! Awa' wi' ye!' in what he imagined to be broad Scots dialect. Then they both flung themselves down on the floor and edged up to their grandmother's chair, hurling questions:

'What else?'

'When'll we go? Does he say a date?'

'What's the place called – Kil something?'

'Kilmorah! Kilmorah! Kilmorah!'

'Would you say it would be a big house, Granny?'

'No, no – it says here *Sarah's cottage.*'

'I guess it's a croft,' said Nan. 'A cottage and a little land. That's the way it is in the Highlands. Did you say Mull? You did – you said the Sound of Mull – way out along the Sound of Mull ... Oh gee – I can't believe it!'

Lucy looked from one to the other with anger and dislike. She turned her back on the lot of them. She stalked off the porch and down the steps, across the grass and into the woodland. There she was out of sight of the house. Then she skirted the far trees and worked back until she could slip into the barn without anyone knowing.

The tall doors were standing open, for the barn was used as a garage. Alan said the place still carried a *sure and savoury smell of horse*. The big Chevrolet was standing as it had stood since Robert Graham took his last trip to Europe. But Nan's little car that she used all the time, to go to school, to go visiting, just to *go out*, was still warm from its last trip. Lucy beat its bonnet with the flat of her hand as she went by, and the blow was meant for Nan.

Lucy went up into the loft. There was a rope ladder. She had made it herself, not very well, and it banged about because the rungs were not all the same length. But she had wanted something she could pull up behind her – it was the only way she could be sure of being alone.

There was still a supply of straw in the loft and it was comfortable and stuffy. Lucy kept there various things that she had grown out of but could not bear to part with. A dolls' house for one. She liked things in miniature and the dolls' house was well equipped. It had belonged to her mother, and it had been Nan's before it became Lucy's. An advantage in being the youngest was that once things reached you they had no farther to go and were yours for keeps. Lucy used the barn when she was sad or angry or just plain sick of the family and needing to be among things entirely her own. Besides the dolls' house there was an aged stuffed monkey with a weary, darned face, and a teddy bear with one eye – he had been that way for years, he looked like a pirate and was always called Henry Morgan. Also her diaries, four of them, mostly without anything written in them. Of the books, the most tattered was *The Wizard of Oz*, but *Rob Roy* ran it pretty close. Best loved of all were the Hallowe'en scarecrows. They came from the road-

side market a few miles outside Winterfield. Each year her father bought her one on his way home from his office in Boston – he never missed a Hallowe'en party if he could help it. The scarecrows had straw bodies, their faces were made of scraps of cotton material and they were mostly about three feet high. One was dressed in the baggy trousers of a clown, and two more had striped skirts and mammy scarves round their heads; and two were witches in pointed hats and pumpkin-colour cloaks. One was called Saphira; she was the second best. The best was named Luciebelle, and there seemed little doubt that she could work powerful magic if she set herself to it – Lucy was always a little careful how she expressed herself in front of Luciebelle.

When she had pulled the ladder up through the trap, Lucy went and lay down in the straw. This was a favourite place, for a small pane of glass was let into the roof where it sloped beside her, and she could see the house and watch the family comings and goings. Alan was standing on the porch at this moment – he was calling 'Lucy! Lucy! Lucy!' as though she were a dog late for his dinner. Presently Roderick came out and

46

stood beside him. They hung about there for a moment or two, side by side, looking like twins in spite of the year between them. Then they went into the house again.

Lucy knew she had spoilt things for the others. She had pulled them back from their excitement, from their sudden feeling that their father's marriage was not going to be such a bad thing after all. Now they were quite miserable. She didn't exactly want them to be miserable – but she wanted them to be steadfast. They had agreed with her at the start that this was to be a second Revolution, that they would set about driving out the English as surely as if they were buckling on their swords and rushing into battle at Lexington. But how was any Graham to treat as an upstart one who came, as it were, bearing Scotland in both outstretched hands? It was dreadfully upsetting to the morale when the enemy behaved in such a friendly fashion.

Lucy rolled over and stuck her face into the straw. She felt a bit like crying. This was unusual when she was alone – though she would sometimes indulge in a shameful and babyish tantrum if she was driven to it by

a desire to get her own way, or grab all the family atten-
tion. Because her face was hidden she did not see Nan
come out of the house and cross to the barn.

There was no way up to the loft except by the rope
ladder, which was hauled up out of reach. So Nan stood
in the barn and called. She called and called, and at last
Lucy wriggled across the straw and pulled back the trap
door. She scowled down at Nan.

'Let me alone, can't you. This is my place. This is my
place and no one comes here except by special permis-
sion and invitation.'

Nan stood looking upwards so that her hair fell back
from her face and hung between her shoulder blades.
'Honey,' she began. Lucy knew that soft voice well. At
its softest she found it hard to resist, so she hardened
her heart. Everyone knew that Nan had their mother's
voice. She had been a Southerner so Nan was always
using words like *Honey*, and even *Landsake*s and *You-
all*.

'What do you want?' demanded Lucy.

'Come on down. I want to talk with you.'

'You just want to bawl me out,' cried Lucy.

'I do not. I just want to have a conversation.'

'A conversation takes two. I'm not talking.'

'That's a low mean way to speak to your only sister,
Lucy Graham. You'll be sorry.'

'Oh sure – when you're dead, I suppose?'

'You'll be sorry right now. This very day. This very
afternoon.'

Lucy stared at Nan. 'Come again?' she said rudely.

'Oh no – if you like it that way, that's the way it can
be. Don't say I didn't warn you.'

'What are you talking about – warn me? What's the
warning, for pete's sake? Nan!'

For Nan had turned and walked away across the beaten earth floor of the barn. Already she was moving into the wedge of sunlight cutting through the open door.

'Nan! Wait, can't you!'

'Why should I? I've said my say.'

'*Nan!* A warning's got to be *about* something!'

'That's right – it has, too.'

'Why don't you talk sense?' shouted Lucy, red in the face.

This time Nan did not reply. She went out of the shadowy barn into the sunshine and never once looked back.

Muttering and shivering with rage and misery, Lucy flung the rope ladder through the trap and started to climb down. She was in such a hurry that she let the ladder swing against the wall, scraping her wrist.

'That's right – bleed!' she snarled, pausing to lick the graze.

She flung herself off the last rung, twisted her ankle and recovered, and pelted after Nan.

But her sister had vanished, and when Lucy hurled herself up the steps on to the porch there was only Mrs Graham there, moving about in a tidying-up manner that seemed dangerously significant.

'What's going *on* in this house?'

'Didn't Nan tell you?'

'No – Nan certainly did not tell me.'

Her grandmother paused and stood still, looking at Lucy coldly.

'Or you wouldn't listen? You're going to have to grow up, Lucy Graham – you're going to have to grow up mighty soon.'

Lucy wore a poker face.

'You know what Alan always says?' her grandmother reminded her. ' "Kid sisters are fine while they're kids." But you've surely got to set about growing up pretty quick, Lucy. I'm warning you.'

'That's the second warning, then. But I never did hear what Nan's was supposed to be about.'

'After you flounced off we suddenly looked up the date on your father's letter. It's taken a long time to get here – nearly twice as long as it should. Right now, he and Sarah must be driving up from Idlewild, and I guess they'll get here in another two hours or so. Could be less. If I were you, I'd go change my dress. And Lucy – one more thing. Why not try changing that mean face you've been wearing lately?'

'Why should I?' snapped Lucy, her heart thumping with fright at the news. 'Why should I? *Why should I?*'

'I just thought you might like your father to recognize you, that's all.'

'Oh of course I'd like it . . . Granny . . . !'

'All right,' said Mrs Graham, as Lucy's voice cracked. 'Get on with you, you silly girl. Make yourself pretty. Make yourself pretty for everybody's sake. Mine, too.'

Lucy turned and fled.

4 | Kilmorah

Murdo was waiting on the quayside when the ferry tied up at Inverloch. Nicholas spotted him when they were only half-way across the loch, moving steadily over the dark smooth water, with a bright sun dipped far enough to give the light a magical clarity.

Nicholas waved wildly when he saw Murdo, but ashore no one answered the wave. Ten or twelve people were waiting for the ferry and there was a line of cars drawn up for the return journey. The hotel and the post office store, the garage and the petrol station, even the bank which opened in a cottage parlour three times a week, had the usual air of waiting for travellers to arrive or to depart. And those who watched the boat had the same air about them. But they would not wave or shout a greeting yet. There was a constant coming and a going here, a setting out and a putting in, and no one could be for ever calling *Welcome* and *Good-bye*. Only when the ferry slid in against the ramp would the tableau break up into movement and sound. The end board would slap down with a rattle of chain and everybody would start shouting.

'Nearly in,' said Charlotte. She looked sideways at her brother, and he turned to her at the same moment. Their faces split into nervous, excited grins. Soon they would greet Murdo. Soon they would pile into his old car and set off, battering him with questions which he would answer slowly and easily and in the strictest order. His name was Murdo Johnstone, which was rather too ordinary to please the two Latymers. They liked to call him *The MacMurdo* – as though he were a clan chief. And this caused him embarrassment, but pleased him, too.

As Nicholas and Charlotte stepped ashore, Murdo came towards them.

'Here you are, then.'

'Here we are – thank goodness,' cried Charlotte. 'It's years – it's *hundreds* of years since we saw you.'

'Ay,' he agreed. 'It's a matter of some months.'

'Are you having a good summer, Murdo?' Nicholas asked. 'It's a wonderful day the day.' He said *the day* instead of *today* in order to sound a bit like a Scot. 'The sky looks good. Are we in for a fine spell?'

'I wouldn't be too certain one way or the other. The glass is going up, and the wind's set fair. You might call it a good spell and not be mistaken ... Where's your baggage? Your mother wrote Alison she'd be along in a day or two.'

'Next week.'

'Have you heard the news, Murdo?'

'I have. I like fine the name she's chosen.' He picked up two of the suitcases, Nicholas took a third and Charlotte gathered up all the half dozen packages they had filled with things they could not bear to be without.

'For that matter, there was a piece in the *Gazette*, that they had in the pub.'

'Goodness! About the wedding?'

'About Mistress Latymer getting married, and how all her friends, and they were many in these parts, would wish her happiness. On the day of the ceremony,' Murdo said, 'her health was drunk by all in the bar at that time. And they were many.'

'Oh she'll like to hear that!' Charlotte cried.

'It was done by the express wish of Rab MacIver, and it was all on the house. But if Rab had had no thought of it, if it had not been on the house at all,' said Murdo handsomely, 'there was half a dozen of us would have made the suggestion.'

The car was standing against the wall by the post office. It was new. Not new as cars go, perhaps, but new to Murdo. He had painted it himself, a rather unpleasant blue.

'How's Alison?' Charlotte asked, when the baggage was stowed in the boot and they were climbing in. 'How's Mrs Mackintosh? What happened about Elsa's young man – the one her mother didn't like? Is Rory married? Did Margaret have a girl or a boy, or was it really twins? Will you be going to the Games this year?'

Murdo worked through the questions in his usual way.

'Alison's blooming.' Alison was his wife, Margaret his married daughter who lived in Edinburgh. 'Mrs Mackintosh has a wee twinge of rheumatism just now. Elsa ran away with that boy from Glasgow and her mother's wishing she'd not been so much against Tam James. Rory's broken it off again – what would you think of that? That's the fourth girl's heart he's broken

– if they break that easy. After all the fuss, Margaret had the wee-est small girl you ever saw – with wispy hair near rowan colour. And as for the Games – Murdo gave his slow smile. 'I'll go if you'll go with me.'

Charlotte leant back in her seat with a huge contented sigh. The MacMurdo never let them down. Listening to him, she could forget the difficulties ahead. He knew everything about everybody and was ready to tell it all, and he never forgot the classic answer to her question about 'the Games'. He had made it first when she was a small girl of six or seven pestering him with her devotion. He had a young daughter himself so he knew all about children, and his patience with her was wonderful to remember. Still, it must have been a relief for him when she transferred her affections to the Alexanders' fat pony.

'MacMurdo for ever!' said Charlotte now. He looked sideways at her and chuckled. They understood one another perfectly.

From the ferry at Inverloch to Kilmorah was a matter of forty miles. It was the slowest and the best part of the long journey north. There were times on the way by train when it seemed as though Kilmorah existed in a land of the imagination and could never be reached by ordinary means. But once they were over the ferry they felt they were home. The road ran the greater part of the way by water, by the lochside and then along the Sound towards the open sea. Once it crossed a neck of land along a glen, but even then the river kept it company. And once it soared along a mountain side and you could look down over bare scree to the twist of the coast mapped-in below. All the way the road was a single track with scooped-out passing places. Drivers grew accustomed to judging the distance, knowing where to pull in and wait for the car coming in the opposite direction. Of course there were some who played false – but even summer visitors picked up the local code in a day or two.

Sometimes the road lifted itself from the water's edge so that you looked down through trees to the blue loch, and then birds sailed beneath you – they might be gulls and kittiwakes and cormorants, or a briefly hovering hawk. In the fine summer sunshine as Murdo Johnstone drove Charlotte and Nicholas to Kilmorah, the heather lay over the hillsides in pools and lakes of colour, and there was colour beginning in the rowan berries on the fine trees, so upstanding and yet so delicate, that stood back to let the road go through. Across on the far shore the outlines were blurred by a haze of summer heat. It was now late afternoon and shadows were blackening in the deep water.

'Alison's been working at your place like a mad thing,' Murdo told them. 'Euan gave a hand with the garden and there's a bed of lettuce you'll like fine to see. Two days since, we'd a gale threatened us, and Euan was all for covering up the stuff with his auntie's best bedcover.' Euan was Murdo's nephew, who lived with them.

'Last year it was a row of peas he tried to keep going,' Charlotte said. 'Do you remember? He took the curtains off the line that Alison had just hung out to air, and made a sort of screen.'

'He's aye a wee bit soft in the head,' said Murdo, but without any malice. He and Euan were a good partnership when it came to fishing and suchlike activities – no one handled a boat better than Euan Macphee.

'So everything's going along just the same as always,' said Charlotte, with deep satisfaction.

'All but one. Did your mother not tell you the old man died?'

'Poor old Angus. Yes, she did.'

'He went up the mountain side one morning like any other morning. And he sat on the stone where he always sat. He sat with his two hands on his stick, like any other day of the summer-time. There was just the difference; he didn't come down. But he had a good sight for his eyes at the last,' said Murdo. 'Aye, it was a good sight out over the ocean, and just a hint of the Cuillins through mist. He'd have wanted no better. We have his granddaughter now, in the croft. Mistress Monroe. A nice enough woman. A widow with one son.'

'What's he like?'

'He's just a wee boy with freckles,' Murdo said, dismissing Mrs Monroe's son.

They had reached that point where the road swung inland briefly, and Kilmorah was suddenly close at hand. The smell of the sea came to them, the feeling of beaches washed by the wide Atlantic. The far shore, which was the Island of Mull, receded as the Sound opened up into the immensity of the ocean. Charlotte and Nicholas fell silent, and Murdo seemed to respect this, for he contented himself with a gentle whistling. Then suddenly they rounded the head, where the ruin of the castle stood out on its spit of land, and there was the village – the church, the hotel, the post office, the farm, the scatter of crofts that pushed on towards the shore.

At last they had reached Kilmorah.

Murdo stopped the car outside the post office.

'I've a call to make on Donald. Run on to your home. The door's open, Alison said to tell you. I'll bring the bags later.' He held the car door and jerked his head along the road towards the shore. 'Be off before anyone sees you and comes rushing. They've a great mind to hear about your mother's new husband.'

Without waiting to thank him for his tact and understanding, they fell out of the car and began at once to run.

For several miles back the surface of the road had been worsening. Now the tarmac became broken and weedy along the stretch between Donald MacIver's garage and Mrs Macdermot's whitewashed cottage. Then again it changed and the surface was gravel carelessly laid. That took you up the hill. From the summit you saw the coastline open up, with the smudge of Skye to the north and the other islands vaguely seen – Coll and Tiree to the south-west, Mull due south, with the town of Tobermory showing along the coast.

Nicholas and Charlotte paused there, as they always did – not speaking, but each making a quick check over the enormous panorama of sea and shore, as though to make certain that nothing had been shifted in their absence.

And standing there, they could see the cottage that was for them the very core of Kilmorah, of Scotland itself.

'Been whitewashed,' said Nicholas.

'Oh it looks good!'

The fresh whitewash made the thick walls look thicker still. Squat, unadorned, the cottage seemed to bed itself down into the earth like a sturdy bush so strong and supple no wind could break or wither it. Alison had lit the fire, and a wisp of smoke rose above the slate roof into the summer evening sky. A low stone

wall contained the ground which with the cottage and
the cow-sheds made up the croft. There were a few
trees, stunted and misshapen by the sea winds. But in
the lee of the building could be seen the garden cared
for by Euan Macphee, with the vegetable patch in the
most sheltered spot, and a flurry of colour at the foot of
the cottage walls, where Euan had grown bright easy
things that endured the salty air – nasturtium and
poppies, blue thistles and marigolds.

'Come on!' Charlotte cried.

She ran on fast, with Nicholas at her side. Here even
the gravel ended and road became sand and shell. But it

was hard beaten and showed tyre marks, for Murdo
drove back and forth at all hours from his own croft
that was still nearer to the shore.

The gate in the wall stood open and so did the front
door – Alison knew the best way to greet them. There
was a kettle pulled to one side of the old-fashioned grate,
just gently steaming. On the round table in the window,
tea was laid on a check cloth, with bannocks and scones
and dark rich fruit cake, a square of pale butter and a
honeycomb. And in the centre of the table was a flat
dish filled with moss stuck with bits of wild honeysuckle
– Alison was good at that sort of thing, she had won a

prize once, at a show in Fort William, and she took great pride in the matter. The peat fire, gently warming the old bones of the place, smelt less of smoke than of comfort and home-coming.

'Sometimes when I'm away,' Charlotte said, 'I wonder if this place is as glorious as I think.'

'And is it?'

'Is it! You're hopeless!'

Nicholas only grunted. It was always easier for Charlotte to express what she felt than it was for him. He was most often flippant when Charlotte wanted him to be serious.

So he said now: 'Old girl, it's not 'arf bad.'

She snatched up the tea cosy and hurled it at him, and it sailed through the open doorway.

'So you're back,' said a voice. And Alison Johnstone stood there with the tea cosy in her hand.

'Alison!' Charlotte rushed to fling her arms round Alison's neck. 'Isn't it wonderful? Isn't it wonderful?'

'That I should be seeing you again?'

'That we should be *here* again!'

'It's a marvel,' agreed Alison. 'And what about all the news? You've a pack of that to be telling, haven't you?'

'I suppose we have.'

'You should have heard the talk, the day the news reached Kilmorah! Not a body in the place but wished your mother the happiness that's owing her. A Graham, too. And he'll be a happy man, for she's as bonny as a lass still. Tell me, now – is he good enough for her? Is he handsome? Is he a kind-hearted man, would you say?'

'We only met him at the wedding,' Charlotte said. 'We haven't had time to find out about his heart.'

Alison looked from one to the other. She frowned a little, uncertain of their mood, her pleasure and excitement suddenly checked. 'You've never quarrelled over the business? You know fine how she deserves her happiness.'

'Of course we haven't quarrelled. And he *is* handsome. It's just that we don't know him properly yet.'

'However,' said Nicholas, 'this will shortly be remedied. He'll be here in a day or two for all the summer holidays. Sorry – va-cation.'

Alison still frowned. 'Aye – six weeks is a fairish time.'

'Also,' Nicholas said, using his smooth, silky voice, the one Charlotte and their mother really hated, 'also, dear Alison, his children. We shall have six whole weeks to learn to love his little ones.'

'So he's a family man?' said Alison cautiously.

'He is *four times* a family man.'

'Losh,' said Alison. 'Four.' For a second she was on their side – then she recovered herself. 'Well, this place is over big, I've always said.'

'So you see, we'll be outnumbered, two to one.' Nicholas looked sideways at Alison. 'What are you thinking?'

Alison flushed up to the roots of her hair. 'I'm thinking I don't at all fancy your manner of speaking. Would you say you're a wee bit ungenerous, or would you not? How many years have you had this place to yourselves – and why wouldn't you be sharing it now? How many long, long years has your mother toiled on her own for you two – and now you grudge her the happiness that's come to her . . .'

Nicholas said, still in his beastly voice: 'Alison doesn't love us any more.'

Charlotte was very pale. She was torn between anger that Alison did not understand and sympathize, and the shock of her disapproval. She had the same warm affection for Alison as for Murdo, and the scorn and disappointment in her voice hurt horribly.

'I came here to congratulate the both of you for your mother's sake,' Alison went on relentlessly. 'I feel a fool.'

'But, Alison – surely you can see? We don't mind Sarah getting married – of course we don't! But couldn't she just have chosen a *childless* widower?'

For a moment, Alison said nothing. Nicholas, watching his sister rather coldly, saw that Alison would have liked to put her arms round the girl and comfort her. When at last she replied, her voice had something like its usual warm tone.

'Whisht, now – whisht. There's a grain of sense in you, I suppose. But what about them – all four of them? Doesn't it come into your mind now and then that they might be feeling the same? I can almost hear them. I can almost see their faces, as they turn from one to the other. Couldn't he just have chosen a *childless* widow?'

For a moment there was a startled silence. It was Nicholas who broke it. He said in a voice more like his own than any he had used since the wedding:

'We asked for that. We've been sticking our necks out, Charley.'

'I just don't expect Alison to be the one who chops them off!' cried Charlotte. And she burst into tears at last. 'Nothing will ever be the same again at Kilmorah!'

'That's the truth,' Alison agreed. 'But away with you now, you foolish lass – did you never hear of a change for the better?'

Of course Alison was absurdly optimistic – they both knew that. But her good sense was just what they needed. They responded eagerly – perhaps things really would turn out better than they feared. For the first time they thought a little of the Grahams themselves. When they considered it, they decided that things might be harder for them. Apart from the surprise, and no doubt the shock, of their father's marriage, they were being hauled across the Atlantic to a strange country. At Kilmorah they would have nothing of their own but their clothes. It was a sobering thought.

'I think I'd better let the two girls have my room,' Charlotte decided, 'and take over the spare room.'

Nicholas looked at her. 'You're not being just the least bit sacrificial?'

'Of course not. Anyway, I've always liked the spare room. It's got the best view of the sea.'

Even if she was making a bit of a sacrifice, Charlotte decided, it made her feel better. She spent a long time changing the furniture around. When she had done it she decided that the room really needed new curtains.

'Couldn't we dash to Fort William and buy some material? Alison would help me make them up.'

'Someone's got to go to Fort William anyway,' Nicholas said. 'We'll have to pitch the tent for the two boys, or one of them anyway – we can't squeeze them both into the room in the roof, they'd stifle. The ground sheet's perished – so we'll have to get another.'

As it happened, Murdo was wanting to go to the town for supplies of one kind and another, so the arrangement was easy to make. He and Nicholas did the practical shopping, while Charlotte and Alison looked for curtain material. It took Charlotte a long time to choose what she wanted, even though the selection was not enormous.

'If only I knew whether they are *flowery* girls or *stripey* girls.'

In the end she picked out neither the one nor the other, but a pattern of seagulls on a blue ground – which Alison said was more suited to a bathroom.

'But why? Just because there's water in a bathroom ... And it isn't salt water, anyway. Think how glorious it'll be when the windows are open and the curtains flap in the wind – there'll be a great crowd of birds against the sky.'

That evening, Charlotte and Alison stitched and stitched, and in the morning they were able to hang the curtains at the bedroom windows.

'Maybe you were right,' said Alison, standing back to admire the effect. 'You're no fool, Charlotte Latymer.'

This was such high praise from Alison that Charlotte was in a wild mood all the rest of the day.

It was about five o'clock the following afternoon that the familiar car came nosing over the rise and on to the last sandy stretch of road that led to the gate of the croft.

'They're here!' Charlotte started out of the house, but Nicholas caught her by the wrist and checked her. 'Let me go, Nicky! We must be waiting for them. Whatever happens we must be waiting for them!'

'Okay – I know that. I just wanted to say one thing. *Good luck.*'

'Oh yes,' she cried, grabbing at his hand then. 'Good luck to the whole boiling of us, if you ask me! And – *Kilmorah to the end of time.*'

'*Kilmorah to the end of time.*'

For years that had been a kind of password for

solemn occasions. Once it was spoken, they ran out of the cottage together and stood at the gate, waving wildly – as though this was the most exciting moment of their lives.

If Alison was watching from her own garden gate, as she probably was, she might feel proud of them . . .

The big estate car pulled up. It seemed to Charlotte and Nicholas to be crammed with strangers – like a bus passed on a country road far from home. For a second, even their mother looked unfamiliar. But only for a second. Then they had wrenched the door open and pulled her out, flinging their arms round her so that she was almost smothered.

One by one the strangers dismounted from the bus and stood waiting. Robert, who had been driving, had his arm round one thin pretty girl, his hand on the shoulder of a skinny crew-cut boy of about twelve. Behind him stood the second boy, the second girl.

Over her mother's head, Charlotte saw them standing there and at once their reserve and isolation in this well-loved place filled her with a totally unexpected warmth. There they stood, waiting to be greeted. Robert was waiting, too. With tact and good humour he had stood back from Sarah's reunion with her own son and daughter. He was smiling, and yet he looked somehow as unsure as his children.

Charlotte stood for the merest second, waiting for her own impulse. Then it came and she knew what to do. She ran forward with her arms outstretched. She cried: 'Robert! Robert!' and hurled herself at him, flinging her arms round his neck and as it were scattering the two who stood close to him. 'It's wonderful to see you! Oh doesn't Sarah look pretty in that dress? Did you choose it?'

Robert gave her a terrific hug that almost took her breath away. Then he pushed her back and stood with his hands on her shoulders, beaming with pleasure at her greeting.

'Well, what a day this is! *What* a day this is! Come on, now – let's do some introducing.' He left one arm round Charlotte, and with the other he pulled in the elder of his two girls. 'This is Nan. Nan – this is Charlotte.'

'Hullo,' said Nan. 'Looks like you've gotten yourself another daughter, Daddy.' She gave Charlotte a cool half-smile. 'He always did say two was enough,' she said.

5 | Grahams and Latymers

Nan lay on her bed and groaned. 'I didn't mean it that way. I didn't. I didn't, Lucy.'

'You sure made it sound that way. The way you made it sound was like you were me – not you.'

'I was scared. Anyone can say crazy things when she's scared.'

'Well, it's done now,' said Lucy. 'Ain't nothin' gonna take it back.'

'Oh Lucy – don't talk like a hobo!'

'They make me feel like a hobo. They really do. And what's awful is – I don't think they mean to one bit. They just *are* that way. Ain't nothin' gonna change them, sister.'

'*Lucy!*'

'Anyway, you can't go on and on day after day having a headache and staying on your bed.'

'I'll be okay soon.'

Lucy looked down at her and grinned. 'Oh jolly good!' she said. And her voice was so nearly Nicholas's voice that Nan burst out laughing.

It was two days since the Grahams had arrived at Kilmorah. Two days since the awful silence that had greeted Nan's remark as she and Charlotte stood in Robert's warm embrace and faced one another for the first time.

That had been a bad moment – almost the worst Lucy could remember. It had been bad because of what Nan had said – worse because Nicholas had butted in. 'Well, I promise he needn't think he's got a third son to bother with,' Nicholas had said. He had laughed as he spoke. In a way, if you just took the laugh and reacted to that, as all of them but Nan tried to do, then Nicholas could be said to have saved the day. But Charlotte had wrenched herself away from Robert and rushed indoors, and Sarah had gone after her, while Nan hung on to her father and looked for a moment as though she might be going to faint or something … Lucy was certainly never going to forget that moment.

Fortunately Murdo and Alison Johnstone had come along the track from their own croft, and there had been more introductions – this time of the very best sort.

'Graham is a good name to bring back to the Highlands,' Murdo had said to Robert. 'You are truly welcome to Kilmorah. Montrose is still remembered.'

It sounded just about as romantic as anything these particular Grahams had ever heard. So romantic, indeed, that Robert had looked rather sharply at Murdo, as if he thought his leg was being quietly pulled. Then he smiled and took the remark at its face value.

'It'd be a fine thing if I could claim that descent,' he had replied. 'Believe me, Montrose is remembered many thousand miles from here.'

Lucy wished he had said 'over the water', which would somehow have fitted the moment, even if they were speaking of a Graham not a Stuart . . .

No one was indoors as Lucy, leaving Nan still on her bed, went downstairs that second afternoon in Kilmorah. The place was utterly quiet except for a ticking clock. On the wall as she crossed the living-room to the door, Lucy saw two paintings – she knew already that they were Sarah's work. One was a dark, rather frightening picture of a storm over this coast – the other was a portrait of the former owner of the croft, known already to Lucy by name. If Aunt Mag had been just as Sarah had painted her, Lucy thought she must have been a very wonderful person. And Sarah must have caught an exact likeness – because Sarah was a very wonderful person herself.

This was the strangest happening of all the strangeness of her father's remarriage – that Lucy, who had been so bitterly hostile to the whole idea, was the one of them all who had accepted Sarah the moment she met her – and not in any grudging way. Sometimes Lucy tried hard to remember her own mother. But it was all so far away, and she had been so young at the time of the accident – sometimes it seemed as though everything before that day had happened to someone else. So that the very instant Lucy had looked at Sarah, that first day when everything had seemed so absolutely awful, she had known that this part of the business, at least, was absolutely right.

As she stepped into the little parlour, Lucy paused again. Everything was interesting at the moment, and with the rest out of the way she could prowl about quite safely. There was a framed photograph on the table by the window that she had tried to look at before – it was so like Nicholas, and yet it was not Nicholas, it was someone older. Of course – it was his father. She looked at it in fascination. This was what Nicholas would be like one day – she seemed almost to be telling his fortune. It must be nice for him to be so like his father, she thought. Perhaps if she were like her mother, she might remember her a little.

Lucy left the photograph and went on out of the front door. She was surprised still by the lack of a porch and the feeling that the house was somehow a part of out-of-doors. She went slowly down the track. Then she stopped and ran indoors again, and came out with her bathing-suit and a towel. She knew she would find the others on the shore and she did not intend to let a fine day go by without a swim.

It was three o'clock and the sun was strong and hot. No one was in sight. There were five or six parked cars among the dunes, which meant visitors somewhere along the shore. Dazzling against the clear blue sky, a couple of seagulls drifted without effort above Lucy's head. Because she was alone and because her bare feet made hardly a sound on the sandy track, Lucy felt as though she moved in a dream. Everything was so extraordinary and yet somehow so expected. She might have been walking on this track towards the sea every day for years, she seemed to know her way so well.

As she passed the next croft, with a footbridge over a stream at its gate, Lucy saw a small boy sitting on the wall. He watched her as she approached, and as she went by he drummed with his bare heels against the wall.

'You'll hurt yourself,' said Lucy.

He did not reply, but stopped drumming. He smiled – at least he stretched his mouth in a gap-toothed grimace. The sun had bleached his sandy hair till it was the colour of tow. His face was so freckled there seemed barely room for his nose.

'Hi,' said Lucy, turning back a step.

He went on grinning but did not reply.

'Is this your home?' Lucy persisted.

He nodded slowly.

'I like it,' she told him. 'I think it's cute. That little old bridge 'n everything. D'you know where I live?'

Again he nodded.

Lucy said slyly: 'Where?'

He pointed along the track.

'That's right. That's where I live. That's my home,' she told him. And as she said it her whole mind and every part of her seemed to jump in astonishment that she could say, even to an unknown small boy, even with her grandmother left behind at High Mount – *That's my home*. It was difficult to know whether she should feel pleased with herself or disgusted. 'What's your name?' she demanded.

As though answering her, his mother at this instant came to the door and called: 'Geordie! Come away in, now.'

The boy looked at Lucy sideways when this happened, and his grin was more teasing than ever.

'Don't you want to know my name?' Lucy demanded. 'Well, I'll never ever tell you till you *ask*.'

His mother stood watching the pair of them, her hand over her eyes against the sun.

'You might be thinking he's soft in the head,' she called. 'But it's just he's verra resairved.'

Lucy waved to Geordie's mother and went on her way. She went through the dunes, the coarse marram grass whipping at her ankles, then found herself on the little path that led up to rising rocky ground, the landward end of a reef that thrust two arms into the sea. From the highest point she could look along the shore to north and south. She saw a scattering of people on the sands, a number of children racing and calling at the water's edge. Then she saw her father and Sarah sitting surrounded by rugs and beach-bags and towels and vacuum-flasks – in fact all the clutter that makes

any trip to any beach like the making of a camp. Charlotte was there, too, hunched over a book, sunning her back. Down among the scatter of smaller rocks Lucy saw Alan and Roderick – Roderick had a small crab in his hand. And farther still, standing rather moodily by himself, she saw Nicholas.

'I must be crazy,' Lucy said out loud. 'I must be plumb crazy. What I feel is – *I feel happy!*'

It did seem a little mad, perhaps. For there was so much that had to be worked out between them all and it would surely take a long time. Eight people, nearly half of them strangers, could not be expected to settle down together all that easily – there must be trouble ahead. Yet in spite of this, in spite of the bad beginning, of Charlotte's hostility and Nan's wretchedness, Lucy felt light as air. Looking about her, she just could not decide which of half a dozen pleasant things to do first.

It took her about ten minutes to decide that she would put on her swimsuit, take to the water north of where she now stood, and swim round the little headland of the reef. She could then surprise her father and Sarah by emerging from the waves almost where they were sitting. Lucy was proud of her swimming.

She had soon changed, rolled up her clothes and hidden them under a pile of stones, and was running over the sand to the water.

The sand here was shell sand, so that instead of being merely golden it was streaked and coloured and full of strange lights from blue and green and rosy shells – some big and beautiful, others so minute you could hardly see them, yet still perfect shells. Lucy curled her toes as she walked and the sun made her skin glow. She paused and retied her hair, turning it from a ponytail into a plait that could be looped up in a knob on top of her head, out of the way as she swam. Then she ran on, into the water that was no more at first than a change in texture, turning the sand from warm to less warm, to cool, and then at last to chill. She pulled in her breath and ran on until the sea was dragging at her knees. A few more yards and she was able to plunge in.

Even on that day the cold of the Atlantic made her gasp. She struck out boldly and soon the sun on her head and neck warmed her again, and the water was no longer cold, only soft and buoyant and beautiful.

The Grahams were all good swimmers, but Lucy was the best. Her father had taught her when she was only five, and she had won medals and two silver cups. She had no difficulty in getting herself round the little headland into the triangle of water between the reef's two outstretched arms. Already she had a sight of her father and Sarah, unsuspecting and relaxed as they sat together on the shore. It was as she smiled to think how she would surprise them that she was surprised herself. A long swelling wave broke over the tip of the reef and rolled her in between the two arms, in a lazy and apparently friendly fashion. Then it pulled right back again and took her with it.

That saved her trouble, but it carried her much too far. She struck out for the shore confidently enough, then knew in a matter of seconds that she was making no progress at all.

Lucy looked about her but no other swimmers were within reach. In fact she realized at once that they were all either north or south of the reef, as though they knew the difficulties of the water in between. For a moment she panicked, feeling like a cork in the deceptively gentle sea, knowing all too well how easily she might be swept farther and farther out – terrifyingly aware that no one even knew she was there.

She rested and steadied herself before trying again. Resting was not a good thing in one way, for the moment she relaxed she was swept helplessly on the swell. She closed her eyes tight for a second and tried to draw in strength and good sense to herself. She could not believe that this was happening to her, and even though she was frightened she managed to be angry, too, at her own stupidity.

'Can you manage?' asked a voice at her shoulder.

Lucy opened her eyes and found Nicholas close beside her.

'I guess I'm glad to see a friendly face,' she replied.

'Let the swell take you for a bit. You can kick out of it beyond the second reef.'

What made Lucy want to laugh was his conversational tone – as though they had met at a tea party or somewhere and he was showing her round the garden. At once she felt twice herself, she felt strong and full of breath and her fright went out of her.

'Ought to have warned you,' Nicholas said. He swam beside her, strongly and easily, going with the swell, and she followed his example. 'I must say, old girl,' he remarked casually, 'you're a jolly good swimmer.'

Lucy flushed inwardly, laughing at the words because they were 'so English', yet pleased with their flattery. The ocean, which had seemed so enormous, became much smaller because she was sharing it with Nicholas.

'Now,' he said at last. 'Bit of an effort here and we're clear. I'll show you.'

It was easy for him but less easy to follow. She was swept back again, and again she was terrified. What if he went on, thinking she was following? What if she called and he did not hear? Water gushed up into her face without warning and the greenness of it seemed to engulf her. But at once she felt him grab her and lift her.

'Okay,' he said, very easily, 'leave this bit to me. You don't mind, do you?'

She would never forget that *You don't mind*. It was so tactful and wise. She rolled on to her back at once and he took her over the difficult bit as strongly and effortlessly as if he had only just got into the water and was miles and miles yet from fatigue.

'Now you're all right,' he said after a bit, and let her go.

They swam the rest of the way side by side, reaching the shore in the lee of the rocks, where they were still out of sight of the others. As they reached the dry sand, Nicholas gave Lucy his hand and pulled her up the beach. He had left his towel on the rocks and he tossed it to her.

'Rub down! Go on – harder. Are you cold?'

She shook her head. She looked at him and grimaced. 'Gosh,' she said. 'Thanks.'

'There are one or two difficult bits on this stretch of coast. I'll tell you about them sometime. Come on – run! Race you!'

He started to run across the sand and Lucy ran after. The sun seemed to creep back into her bones and she was filled with the wonderful good cheer and well-being that follows a taste of danger. If Nicholas had not been around . . . Well, Lucy intended not to have bad dreams about that. He had been.

Suddenly Sarah was waving and they were waving back. As Lucy ran up the last few yards of the shore she was aware of Sarah's face and of her father's. There was intense pleasure in each of them. It must be that the sight of Nicholas and Lucy running cheerfully side by side had suggested to them that things were on the move between the Grahams and the Latymers.

'Where have you been?' Sarah cried.

Nicholas plumped down and stretched out flat.

'Lucy took me swimming,' he said. 'She's a terror. I'm worn out.'

As he spoke he rolled over on to his stomach and put his cheek against his folded arms. Lucy already had her mouth open to say – what? Something like *Nicholas saved my life*, perhaps. But she saw him looking up at her with his one visible eye and she paused. He was cautioning her and she knew at once that he was right. She would not have bad dreams – there was no point in handing them to the parents.

'The best swim I ever had,' she said.

She looked down at Nicholas. The one eye winked. Then he rolled over and sat up, grinning at her. He was real. He was a real person after all . . .

'Tell you what, Mamma,' he said, moving nearer to Sarah, 'we ought to take all these people on a picnic. To Ardtorquil.'

'Oh, of course! What a wonderful idea, Nicky! What about it, Robert?'

'Sounds swell to me. When'll we go? Tomorrow too soon?'

'I don't see why we shouldn't make it tomorrow,' Sarah said. 'While the fine weather lasts.'

Charlotte looked up from her book. 'What about Nan?'

'She'll be okay,' said Lucy.

'Think so?'

'Oh sure – she'll be okay.'

'Did she seem better when you left her?'

'Sure – she's practically cured,' Lucy cried, impatiently.

Charlotte shut her book and got up lazily.

'I've got things I want to do. I'll go up now, I think.'

As she left in one direction, Alan and Roderick came up from the other, from the water's edge, looking as usual more like one boy than two. Roderick was carrying the crab.

'Hey, Lucy – did you bring a pail?'

'Now, would I? A pail and shovel? I'm not a baby!'

'We need a pail of salt water,' Roderick complained. 'How're we going to keep 'm alive if we don't have one?'

'Let him go back to the sea,' said Nicholas. 'Easy.'

'Never mind about crabs,' their father said. 'Come on

over here, you two. We're debating picnics. Tomorrow's the day. How about it?'

The two boys stood and stared at Robert.

'Here?'

'No – no. Where's the sense of a picnic in your own backyard? Somewhere up the coast – isn't it, Nicholas?'

'A few miles. Ardtorquil. It's a very lonely place. You have to know how to get there.'

'It's always been our favourite place,' Sarah said. 'I don't believe we've ever told anybody about it before – have we, Nicky?'

He answered very shortly: 'No. Never till now.'

'Well – okay,' said Alan.

'Swell,' said Roderick.

Nicholas glared at them. 'Don't come if you don't want to. There's no compulsion.'

'Oh, sure we want to. We can get on with what we figured on doing tomorrow some other day, I guess.'

'They never shout much,' Lucy said to Nicholas, in a low voice. 'You don't need to take the least bit of notice of those two boys.'

Sarah was not going to be dashed by any sort of disagreement at this stage.

'That's settled, then. Good. Now let's get back home, shall we? Then we can see what food there is and get ourselves organized. It's a lovely sky. I'm sure it'll be fine tomorrow.'

They all walked back to the cottage in a straggling line – Sarah and Robert comfortably arm-in-arm, Alan and Roderick behind them, and last of all Nicholas and Lucy. He walked ahead of her and did not speak, but anyone could see that they were together.

As they came near home, the freckle-faced boy Lucy had spoken to that afternoon appeared from nowhere and tagged along beside her.

At once Nicholas turned and asked: 'Who's your friend?'

'It's Geordie. Don't you know Geordie?'

'He'll be Mrs Monroe's wee boy with freckles, no doubt. He's a newcomer to these parts – aren't you, Geordie?'

Geordie did not answer.

'He doesn't have much interest in conversation,' Lucy said.

Nicholas chuckled . . .

Lucy found herself thinking comfortably – *I have two friends since I left home this afternoon.* She began whistling through her teeth.

'Disgusting noise!' cried Nicholas.

Lucy went on whistling until laughter spoilt it.

When they reached the croft, Nan was in the garden. So, indeed, was Charlotte. They were sitting on the wall – rather far apart, perhaps, but not so far that they could not talk to one another. And they were talking.

Someone had made a very necessary effort. It really didn't matter in the least which one of them it had been . . .

6 | Picnic

Long afterwards, Charlotte said of the morning of the picnic: 'When I woke up I heard the whole house *vibrating* with good intentions!'

Outside in the garden, in the tent shared by Alan and Roderick, the same thing was happening. The two boys lay silent in their sleeping bags, eyes open, hands behind their heads, both thinking the same thoughts – which were thoughts of the day and the picnic and how it had better be good; and so had they. They remained in this state until they heard the back door open.

Charlotte called to them: 'Time, gentlemen!' – an English joke of hers which they failed to understand, though she had said it each morning she called them.

'Okay!' said Alan, loudly.

'Ok*ay*,' said Roderick, under his breath.

Breakfast was bound to be a bit of a scramble, there

were so many of them to be fed, and nobody really knew yet what the others liked. There was a shortage of orange juice because Alison, who had done the marketing, had not catered for American tastes. Then there had to be coffee for Sarah, Nan and Charlotte, but tea for Robert and Nicholas and milk for Alan, Roderick and Lucy. Charlotte had for the past two years been the breakfast-getter at Kilmorah and now she had her hands full. She was glad to see Nan, that morning of the picnic, come down ahead of the others.

'Shall I fix the table, Charlotte?'

'Oh please – yes. Cloth in the dresser drawer. Also napkins. Knives and silver in the righthand small drawer. You'll find sugar and butter and things in the larder.'

It was the first time Nan had offered to help. She frowned in an apologetic way as she listened to these instructions.

'You'll think I'm crazy. Which do you call the *dresser*? It's bedroom furniture back home.'

'Oh you mean – a dressing table? Or a chest of drawers?'

'I guess I mean one or the other while I'm here!'

'Well, that's the dresser this side of the Atlantic,' Charlotte said, pointing it out. 'The china's in the cupboard at the bottom. There isn't really quite enough to go round. We've never been more than four till now – and that was years ago while we still had Aunt Mag.'

'Sarah was telling us about her. She sounded just darling.'

Charlotte stood cutting rind off rashers of bacon and laughing at Nan.

'What's wrong with that?' Nan cried, flushing.

'Nothing! It's just that I don't know whether I've got to learn American or you've got to learn English!'

Just for a second, Nan looked huffed. Then she laughed, too.

'Make it Yankish,' she suggested, and went out of the kitchen to get on with the job of laying the table.

Nan more than any of them knew that nothing must happen to disturb this day's arrangements. This was the first enterprise they had undertaken as a family and much could hang on it. As the eldest, she felt herself responsible for the behaviour of the other three – and so far she was the only one of them who had behaved badly. The boys had done nothing yet to offend anyone in particular, and Lucy was positively enjoying herself. Perhaps in Lucy's acceptance of Sarah lay Nan's greatest difficulty. Hard as she tried, she could not help feeling a fraction jealous – and this was particularly bitter for she had been warm and generous in accepting her father's remarriage, aware of his happiness and glad of it . . .

It was a wonderful morning. Short of space on the round table, Charlotte called to Nan to pull the garden table up close by the open window.

'We can put the boys there and hand food out to them. I daresay they'll like it.'

They did. So did Lucy, who insisted on joining them. Soon they were all seated, five of them inside and three of them out. Everything went to time. Charlotte felt pleased with herself. She could do nothing wrong that morning. The coffee was perfect, the toast made at the kitchen fire by Nan had for once not burnt. The bacon curled just so, the eggs were as gold and as white as eggs in a colour photograph.

Robert was full of praises. 'I see your mother's

brought you two Latymers up to be thoroughly self-
sufficient. You're a mighty good cook, stepdaughter.
And though I say it, Nan's not so bad, either.'

'Oh I'm not that good, Daddy. If I ever have an egg
in a pan, that egg's sure to break.'

'You needn't sound so humble about it,' Charlotte
said ... They do *exaggerate* so, she thought irritably ...

'Anyway, Nan can make whole dresses and she
doesn't break those,' Lucy said from beyond the window.

'Not even if they're white with a yoke?' asked
Nicholas.

Lucy screamed with laughter, but Charlotte looked at
her brother in rather cold surprise. He was always so
lofty and scornful of pun making, what could have
happened to him? Perhaps he was laughing up his
sleeve. But she saw that he was trying – in the same way
that she had been trying yesterday afternoon, when she
left the shore and sought out Nan and started to make
friends. So Charlotte joined in the laughter and gradually they all began to relax. There was so much noise
from eight people all talking together that it sounded
like a party.

Alison was in the kitchen by the time they were
clearing away the breakfast things.

'Leave those, now,' she commanded. 'I've been cutting your sandwiches for the picnic.'

'Alison's the champion sandwich-cutter of all the
bonny Highlands,' Nicholas told Nan.

'As to that,' said Alison, 'I mind my own mother
could slice bread like a machine. But she was canny
with the filling. Look here – I have stuffed them with
meat for you. You'll no starve the day.'

So with Alison's help the organization of the picnic

was completed. Somewhere about eleven they piled into the big car and set off along the track, through Kilmorah itself, and then away to the north-west and Ardtorquil.

Robert was driving.

'You need to leave the car just here, sir,' Nicholas told him, when they came to the place. 'We have to hump the things down to the shore.'

Robert pulled the car off where the track had dwindled away to grass and heather. He turned off the engine and sat absolutely still, his head a little to one side.

'Be quiet and listen, will you . . .'

There seemed little to hear – just the stillness of the summer morning spread over the long unspoilt coastline. And then, like a sound-pattern on the hot hazy sky, they heard the high jubilation of hidden larks. It seemed a shame to break in on the quiet and the birdsong, but they could hardly sit there listening all the rest of the day. And when they got out of the brake and their voices began to ring out, eight of them, all different except for Alan's and Roderick's who seemed to share one between them, the noise was too cheerful to be resented.

Charlotte saw Sarah and Robert exchange a glance and smile. They were pleased and happy and wanted one another to know it.

'We're a whole party, just us without one single soul more,' Lucy said to Sarah. 'I'll carry that. Give me the cushion. Hey – let me have that rug. Who's carrying the big basket? Did you bring the bananas? Charlotte – did you remember the bananas?'

'I left the ban-an-as behind.'

'Oh *there* – gee . . .'

'But I brought the ban-ah-nas!'

Lucy gave her a push and Charlotte toppled. She was carrying the smaller picnic basket and her own beach bag which swung out and cracked against a boulder.

'Oh *Lucy*! That's my *suntan* oil! It's broken! The bag'll be ruined and I shall *blister*!'

'I've got some,' Nan said quickly. 'Have mine. You can have some of mine, honey. Charlotte,' she corrected herself.

They were ahead of Sarah and Robert, who now caught up with them.

'That basket's meant for me or Nicholas,' Robert said, taking it from Charlotte. 'Hello – what's going on here?'

Lucy wailed: 'Oh Daddy – it's *awful* –'

'It's nothing,' Charlotte cried. 'Nothing – nothing – absolutely nothing! Come on, Lucy – help me fish out the bits.'

Lucy put down the immense burden of rugs and towels and various paraphernalia that she had insisted on carrying for Sarah, and went down on her knees to pick the broken bits out of Charlotte's beach bag.

'Lucky I had it in a paper bag, Lucy.'

'I don't see what's lucky –'

'It's lucky about the paper and it's lucky I shan't have splinters of glass in the bathing-suit and it's lucky Nan's got enough oil to lend me some.' And rather belatedly Charlotte smiled at Nan and thanked her.

It was a stiff scramble down the cliff path to the shore. There the white sand stretched in the curve of a shallow bay. There was no living thing in sight but the seabirds along the tide line – gulls and oyster catchers, picking and gobbling, and crowds of sanderling that moved away in a flock so swiftly that they looked like clock-work birds. Out to sea on a half-submerged reef, cormorants stood in rows with their heads into the breeze, and there were scores of gull families, the youngsters screaming and pestering for food.

Robert stood looking round him, with Nicholas at his side.

'I'm no bird man, Nicholas, but I shall remember this place. It was a fine suggestion of yours, that we should come here.'

'It was one of Aunt Mag's places,' Nicholas said. 'There was a seal that used to come here. Aunt Mag was friendly with it – I really mean that – just as if it was a person. She used to come here and whistle and the seal would come up out of the water and hurry to meet her.'

As he spoke, a feeling of protest and misery surged over Nicholas. He could not imagine what had made him suggest this picnic, why Charlotte had accepted the idea. They had never shown Ardtorquil even to the dearest friends who had stayed with them from time to time at Kilmorah. Why had they so stupidly and so lightly allowed this invasion of Grahams to the place? He heard the voices of Lucy and her brothers already shouting at the water's edge and he felt quite desperate. He knew the awfulness of sharing something precious and then discovering that the very sharing has turned it into something different – not worse, necessarily, but quite simply not the same. It was like giving away a treasured possession in a moment of generosity – and then wondering if the gift was appreciated . . .

Charlotte was calling: 'Nicky! Come and look. Roderick's found a sea urchin.'

Nicholas left Robert and joined the others. For the first time he saw Roderick looking pleased and

animated. His face was split by a tight grin, and his cropped hair seemed to be standing up even more than usual. He was better pleased with the urchin even than he had been with the crab yesterday.

'Funny thing,' Nicholas said. 'There are two things I've always wanted to find on the shore – a sea urchin and a green glass fishing float. Believe it or not, I've never found either.'

'Roderick's had beginner's luck,' said Charlotte. She laughed at Nicholas's long face. She had found both herself, time and again, and he had always been rather disagreeable about it, so she did not feel particularly sorry for him this time.

By the middle of the day they had forgotten their good resolutions. That did not mean they were quarrelling, simply that they were suddenly enjoying themselves without trying. They swam and threw a ball, and dug in the sand, and scrambled and climbed, and lay in the sun. Charlotte and Nan carefully oiled themselves and kept turning this way and that – like pancakes on a griddle, Robert said. Then they had their lunch and argued over whether biscuits should be called crackers, as the Grahams called them, or biscuits as the Latymers called them. That led on to a lot of friendly arguments about similar words. Nan said she and Charlotte had decided to speak Yankish in future. Alan and Roderick instructed Nicholas in the mysteries of their school life back home – carefully assuring him that an English public school was the same as an American private one – which on the whole Nicholas had to agree was a more reasonable way to describe them.

It was all so easy. Why had they ever supposed there could be difficulties?

'Where would you be,' Charlotte suddenly asked, 'if you weren't here?'

'Oh we'd be off camping some place,' replied Alan. 'Last year we took the trail over the White Mountains to Mount Washington.'

'Trail! I didn't know you used that word still. It sounds like Indians and Cowboys.'

'That's just what it is! It's all trails back home,' said Roderick. 'There's the Mohawk Trail and the Appalachian Trail ...'

'Oh I wish we had a trail,' Charlotte said. 'What a nuisance!'

'We've got the Road to the Isles,' Sarah reminded her.

'Gee, yes – *that's* something!' cried Alan.

And so gradually it turned into a wonderful party at which every single guest liked every other guest. Once

Roderick had found the sea urchin and allowed himself to be pleased, Alan had been pleased, too. They seemed to become two amused and amusing boys as if by magic – they were no longer the really formidable partnership they formed most of the time, a partnership so tight that it almost seemed they had only one shadow between them.

Surely nothing could go wrong with the day now – and if this day went well, then so might any other . . .

Afterwards, Charlotte insisted she had known all along. The good resolutions of the morning, though they had fallen into disuse by noon, must none the less have worn them all out. About four in the afternoon, something went wrong.

It all began with the Graham tartan.

Few things exasperated Nicholas and Charlotte more than the fact that however fond they were of Scotland and all things Scottish, they were not Scots, nothing could ever make them Scots, they belonged to no clan – and so they were not entitled to wear a clan tartan. Hundreds of times they had stood gazing in shop windows draped with every tartan in the country. Once Charlotte had fallen. Like any ignorant tourist she had permitted herself to buy a scarf in Stuart hunting tartan – and then Murdo had seen her wearing it. He said not a word – but she had found herself instantly on the defensive.

'Can't I just wear it as a *supporter*, MacMurdo? As a staunch Stuart supporter – as a Jacobite? Can't I?'

'I know of nothing in the world can stop you,' he had replied. 'And no doubt, if I should wish, there's none could stop me wearing an imitation of the Queen of England's gold crown.'

Charlotte had sadly unwound the scarf from her neck, crept home and put it on the fire. After that, she and Nicholas had tried hard to discover some relation with Scottish blood, who might help them in this matter. But there was only Great-Aunt Eva, on their

father's side, who had married a Crawford. It just would not work and they had to resign themselves. The worst was over now by several years – they had accepted what had seemed when they were younger to be quite unbearable.

And then, at the picnic at Ardtorquil, the unbearable reappeared.

It was Roderick who began it.

Picnic

'I just thought of something, Pop. Now we're in Scotland we can wear kilts. Could you buy us some, please?'

'Daddy, yes!' cried Lucy. 'All of us. All four. With safety pins 'n everything.'

'You might look a little like a pipe band,' their father objected.

'What's wrong with a pipe band? It'd be such a *little* band. Anyway,' Lucy gabbled, sitting back on her heels and bouncing on them slightly, 'why only four, for goodness' sake? You could buy kilts for *all* your children. For all *six*, Daddy. You could – you could!'

Robert laughed. He pulled Lucy up close to him and hugged her. It was quite clear that he did so not only because she was the youngest and had a particular place in the family, but because she at least had accepted the fact that he really might be said to have six children now.

'Oh-oh,' said Alan, eyeing Nicholas. 'Looks like there's someone here wouldn't want a kilt.'

'Wouldn't you, Nicholas?' Lucy said, amazed.

'No.'

Perhaps he had no more meant to sound so coldly hostile than Nan had meant, on that first evening, to offend Charlotte. As it was, his voice cut down on the chatter and the warmth like a chopper – like a chopper with a blade of ice.

Sarah said quickly to Alan: 'Do you know all about tartans, Alan? I expect you do.'

'Oh sure – we've got a whole huge book about that sort of thing back home. Rod did a school essay on it – won him a prize. Didn't it, Rod?'

'Yeah,' said Roderick, shifting from one foot to the other.

'What was the prize?' asked Charlotte tartly. 'A dirk? A sporran?'

'I don't see why you all have to slap down the boys and Lucy that way,' Nan said. 'People do know about tartans and Scots do wear kilts – anyone knows that. So what's so funny in any of us wanting to?'

'Nothing funny, Nan dear,' Sarah assured her. 'Don't take any notice of my two. They have a kind of mania about Scotland –'

'That's what we've got,' Alan broke in. 'Yes, sir. It's a mania.'

'But you don't have to be a maniac to wear a kilt, I guess,' said Roderick.

'You just have to be a Scot,' said Charlotte. 'It's as easy as that.'

The moment she had spoken, she began to turn uncomfortably red. She looked at Nicholas in a hunted way, and then at her mother.

But Sarah was looking at Robert, who said quietly: 'But, Charlotte, my dear, that's surely what the Grahams are.'

'Well, I don't think so,' she cried, laughing rudely. 'Not these Grahams. I think they're Americans. That's something quite different, if you ask me.'

'In fact I didn't quite do that,' Robert said pleasantly. 'But I look at it this way –'

'Something altogether newer, if you see what I mean,' Charlotte broke in, losing her head completely. 'The people of Scotland are ancient and proud. While the Americans –'

She broke off abruptly, bit her lip, and turned as pale as she had been flaming scarlet.

'Charlotte! For heaven's sake,' Sarah cried,

'pull yourself together. Apologize. Apologize – now. Quickly. Apologize to Robert for what you have just said.'

'Yes, all right,' said Charlotte, overcome. 'I do. I do, honestly. I didn't mean it to sound like that. It really wasn't exactly what I meant to say . . .'

'Forget it,' said Robert. 'How's the time going? What do you say we have one more dip before we get back home?'

Lucy had slid up beside Sarah and Sarah had her arm round Lucy's waist. They both looked oddly frightened. In spite of Robert's carefully even and cheerful tone, nobody moved.

Then Alan said: 'Okay. Only you just say Yes about the kilt first, will you, Daddy?'

'We'll talk about that another time.'

'We're talking about it right now. So why don't we get it over with?'

'Oh for pete's sake, Alan,' his father said. 'Can't you stop nagging?'

'I don't see what's so holy about it –' Roderick began.

'Roderick! Be quiet. That'll do. It's finished. Understand? Definitely over.'

Nicholas jumped to his feet.

'Come on, Lucy. Let's give them a swimming display.'

'I'm okay right here.'

'Go on, Lucy,' Sarah urged.

'I don't want to. I like it sitting just where I am next to you, Sarah.'

A slight whine had crept into Lucy's voice. Because she was disturbed by the way things were going, she felt helpless and flustered and fell back on babyish tricks. But Sarah was flustered, too, and so she took her arm away from Lucy and gave her what was meant to be a light and friendly push. Lucy fell over sideways, banged her head not too hard on a large stone, and burst into wild tears.

Nan rushed to her. 'Honey! Lucy, honey!'

Nicholas said: 'For crying out loud . . .'

It was not meant to be a pun this time. But it sounded like it. Alan punched him.

The punch was utterly unexpected, skilled and painful. Nicholas shouted out in pain – then grabbed Alan in a fury and turned him upside down.

At the same instant Sarah said quite sharply to Nan: 'Really, I don't think all that is absolutely necessary. She hasn't fractured her skull, you know.'

'Ever see a Highland chieftain endways up?' Nicholas said, in a nasty voice, dangling Alan.

'Look out, Nicky!' Charlotte screamed.

But she was too late. Roderick hurled himself at Nicholas, tackling him round the knees. The three boys went down in a shouting struggling mass.

Charlotte began to laugh. Unfortunately, her eyes had filled with tears at the exact moment that the laughter started. She stood there, pointing at the boys, sobbing and laughing at the same time, the tears rolling down her cheeks.

Robert grabbed Charlotte by the arm, shook her hard and slapped her cheek. It was the correct treatment for silly hysteria, but it threw Charlotte into a rage and she hit back.

'That'll do,' he said. 'That'll do.' Then his quiet voice bit at her in sudden and justifiable anger. 'Can't you see you're upsetting your mother?'

All this time, Sarah had been sitting on the rug on the sand, but now she rose. She was very pale. Without looking at any of them, she began walking away fast towards the little track that led up to where the car was waiting. Her hands were clasped in front of her and her head was bowed. She stumbled as she went.

This was worse than anything imaginable and Charlotte cried out in anguish: 'Sarah! Mummy! Mummy!' She tried to run after her mother, but Robert held her back.

'Stay where you are. Do you understand? You've done enough.'

He went quickly and firmly after Sarah, put his arm round her, and went with her up the steep cliffside and out of sight.

By now Lucy was lying flat on her stomach on the rug with her face hidden. The three boys had separated and were mournfully or angrily inspecting their injuries – not very severe. That left Nan and Charlotte to glare at one another.

'Time you all grew up, honey,' Nan drawled.

Charlotte narrowed her eyes. 'Don't tempt me too far – just don't tempt me too far, that's all . . .'

'Oh, shut up, the pair of you,' Nicholas broke in. 'Come on. Let's get packed up. Move, can't you, Lucy? Why do you women have to be so dramatic about everything? Lucy! Get off that rug!'

Lucy got off the rug. She looked under her eyebrows and said nothing. If he had known anything about her he would have known that with that look in her eyes she could only be thinking of the witch scarecrows left behind at High Mount, Winterfield, Massachusetts, where they could unfortunately perform no magic for Lucy against her enemies.

'Go on,' Nicholas snapped at the two boys. 'Pick the things up. Nan – pack up the basket. Charlotte, take the towels and things. Get going. Can't you understand? The picnic's over – finished. If you ask me, it's a pity it was ever thought of. You can blame me for that bright idea. I should have known better. You're none of you to be trusted.'

And to himself he added miserably – *Ardtorquil's done for now . . .*

7 | Crisis and Challenge

Next morning, Charlotte was in the kitchen getting breakfast as usual. She was uncomfortably deep in her own thoughts. She kept trying to decide which of them had been responsible for yesterday's deplorable scene. She could not help knowing that if she had kept her head instead of being so abominably rude to Robert, things might have been kept from reaching such a climax. If Lucy hadn't whined ... If Nicholas's scuffle with Alan and Roderick had not ended in violence ... If

Nan . . . Well, she could continue listing the *ifs* for ever. And much good it would do. There was no escape from the facts of the case and they were not at all pretty seen in the cold light of day, with all the fury and jealousy gone – and nothing but the reckoning to be faced.

Robert, coming suddenly into the kitchen, made Charlotte jump.

'You mother won't be down to breakfast. Let me have a tray, will you?'

'Is she – What's the matter with her?'

'She's not sick, if that's what you're thinking. She just wants to stay peaceful for a while. I think she's got something there. Make it a tray for two.'

Charlotte turned away quickly and began preparing the tray. She kept her back towards him so that he would not see the one shameful tear running over her left cheek and making at speed for the tip of her nose. At last she had the tray ready and handed it to him.

'Robert –'

'Not just now – do you mind? Breakfast in peace, I said, and that's just what I meant.'

By now Nan had arrived and was putting the cloth on the table. Robert did not speak to her, either, but took the tray and went straight back upstairs.

Gradually the rest of the household assembled. It was fine again, so Lucy and the boys sat outside. They were the only ones who talked, but without much spirit. Indoors, Charlotte, Nicholas and Nan got on with their breakfast in silence. Every now and again one of them would say *More coffee?* or *More toast?* or *Marmalade, please*. But it never led anywhere.

They had washed up and got everything cleared away when Robert reappeared.

'Come and sit down,' he said. 'All of you. We have to talk.'

Although he was not looking angry, he had about him the air of a man who had come to some decision after long discussion – and like a man who, having come to that decision, would not allow himself to be moved from it by so much as half a hairsbreadth.

One by one they went into the living-room and slid into places round the table, eyeing him awkwardly. Only Nicholas remained standing, leaning against the dresser in a slightly arrogant way which told Charlotte, if no one else, how uneasy he was feeling.

'Sit down, Nicholas,' said his stepfather, without bothering to look at him.

So Nicholas sat down, making much of settling himself, and then sitting back in his chair with his legs straight out in front of him and his hands stuck into his trouser pockets.

Then Robert took the chair at the head of the table, if a round table could be said to have a head – at least it was the chair he always used, the carver's chair, the one with arms. And suddenly it all seemed like a board meeting, or a council – or even parliament. It was oddly solemn, and there was not one of them who did not feel helpless and rather small. Whatever he might say to them, they would have very little defence, for they all knew how unpardonable their behaviour of yesterday had been.

'I have been giving much careful thought to what happened yesterday,' Robert began in a level voice. 'I have now decided on the best thing to be done – and that is what will be done, make no mistake about it. Maybe it was wrong to arrange this vacation the way I did. I counted on civilized cooperation from my own children, and I think without a doubt Sarah did the same. It could be this was not reasonable thinking in either one of us. I need not ask what any of you is thinking about that. You answered the question, in your own inimitable fashion, yesterday at Ardtorquil.'

He paused and looked round at them. Nan smiled nervously and said 'Landsakes, Daddy!' in a cajoling way she knew to be effective – but it took no effect today.

'It could be,' Robert went on, in his lawyer's manner, 'you were sure to squabble and wrangle like a lot of spoilt brats.' For the first time his voice snapped a bit, and Nicholas looked up quickly and seemed about to break in – then thought better of it. 'Parents do sometimes try their children too far, I guess,' Robert said. 'But that's because they rate them pretty high.'

Again he paused and looked round at them. Charlotte was sitting blinking at her folded hands. Nan was still trying to win him with a gentle, puzzled expression; and failing utterly. Alan and Roderick were sharing a chair, tilting it on to its back legs and looking detached from what was going on. Lucy had her elbows on the table and her face on her fists. Nicholas had not moved from his original position, and his eyes never left Robert's face.

'The point as I see it is simply this,' Robert went on. 'Sarah has done me the honour of marrying me. This can only mean that I become responsible for her children as well as my own. Therefore, from my position of authority over every one of you, I say this: I will not endure that my wife be subjected to the kind of hoodlum behaviour you all saw fit to indulge in at Ardtorquil. That is over. As from today, that will not happen again. Now – is that clear to you all?'

He looked round the table as though expecting a reply. But they could only nod or mumble a *Yes*.

'Well, then, in view of all this, I find myself with only one course open to me – and that after due discussion and consultation with Sarah I intend to take.' He looked briefly at his watch. 'It is now somewhere around eleven. At fifteen or so of twelve, my wife and I will be leaving Kilmorah.'

Nicholas thrust back his chair as though he was going to leap shouting to his feet – then he paused. The others cried out in one way or another, gabbling together – yet too shocked to make any reasonable protest.

'We shall be making a trip farther north,' Robert said. 'We may be away three to four weeks.'

Nicholas managed: 'I don't understand –'

'Now, Nicholas, you're an intelligent boy. I am taking your mother away from here. I submit this is a highly reasonable line of conduct. It is my devout hope – and I know it's hers, too – that by the time we return to Kilmorah our children will have learned how to live together.'

'But, Daddy!' Nan beat her hands on the table. 'You can't do that! You just can't do that to us! I won't stay here without you!'

'Nan, you are sixteen years old and you will still do as I tell you to.' He looked at Charlotte. 'You don't say anything, Charlotte.'

'I don't know what to say . . .' She turned in her chair, so that her hair fell forward and her face was hidden from him. She felt crushed. She knew that this could not happen without her mother's agreement, and that she could only have agreed if she were feeling completely overcome by yesterday's performance. There was nothing particularly distressing about being left on their own – in other circumstances it could have been rather fun, for they all knew about looking after themselves, But Charlotte wondered how she would ever get over the feeling that they had actually driven Sarah and Robert away. She was old enough and sensible enough to realize that even when they were away their parents would not be able really to enjoy themselves – they would be wondering all the time how things were going at Kilmorah, and regretting the failure of the summer holiday they had looked forward to. 'Oh what a mess . . .' she said half to herself, sighing. She looked at Robert. 'You really mean it, don't you?'

And he answered, not sternly, but firmly and gently: 'Yes, Charlotte my dear. I do.'

Nan was now twisting and picking at her handkerchief and trying not to cry. Alan had pulled out a packet of gum and handed it to Roderick. Now they sat there on the shared chair, chewing and gazing at the ceiling.

Nicholas was silent, and Lucy was silent. Even those who knew her best – and all but one of those, her grandmother, were there in the room with her – had not the least idea what Lucy was thinking at that moment. She still had her elbows on the table, her chin in her hands. She had made no move at all, except to shut her eyes tight.

'Now I want to speak of practical matters,' Robert said. 'I'm going to arrange for you to draw on the bank at Inverloch – that's the nearest, your mother tells me, Nicholas. I'll fix that on our way through. Have Murdo drive you there – we'll be leaving the brake, since his little old car won't hold you all. We shall hire a car someplace.' He took out his wallet and removed a slip of paper. 'These are the hotels we shall stay at, with the dates. You can always get in touch if anything should occur that Murdo or Alison are not competent to deal with. I'll be speaking to them . . . Nan – take the addresses – you're usually sensible. Nicholas is the one who knows best about this place and its ways, so I guess he's got to be the one in charge. You see that, don't you, Nan?'

'Oh sure I see. I see a darn sight more than I like to,' Nan complained.

'Charlotte – your mother says you'd better have charge of the cooking. Okay?'

Charlotte nodded. She wouldn't mind that at all. She thought darkly that the rest of them had better treat her civilly or she would reduce their rations. Inside herself, to her own great surprise, she laughed suddenly. The feeling of cold sorrow had begun to go and she felt altogether more like herself.

'I guess that covers everything,' Robert said. 'Any questions?'

No one spoke.

'That's just fine, then. Will someone go find Murdo for me?'

Lucy jumped up and ran off fast. She did not look at Robert or any of them. She slammed the door, then the gate. Geordie Monroe was sitting on the wall, but Lucy went by without giving him a call.

At a quarter to twelve Murdo drove up to the gate in his bright blue car. In silence, Nicholas and the other two boys fetched out the luggage.

Upstairs, Charlotte was knocking on her mother's door.

'It's me! Can I come in?'

Sarah opened the door. It was useless to pretend that she looked anything but intensely unhappy. Charlotte's feeling of guilt and responsibility half choked her for a second. Then she put her arms round Sarah.

'It's the best thing,' she said cheerfully. 'Robert's absolutely right. We're a lot of beasts and we deserve to be locked up and starved.'

'Oh no, darling...'

'True. I don't know what got into me yesterday. I

must have suddenly gone mad. The others were just as bad ... Look – don't worry. We'll manage beautifully – it'll do us all good.'

'I think you will ... I feel you may get along better without us ... Perhaps ... Do you think so?'

'Well – now you've put the idea into my head.' Charlotte laughed and kissed Sarah first on one cheek and then on the other. 'Go away and enjoy yourself.'

'Will you take special care of Lucy? She's very young to be left like this. But Robert says she's tough.'

'She's tough all right. I'll see she's looked after – if Nan gives me the chance.' And again she said, in a commanding voice: 'Go away and *enjoy yourself.*' She felt as she had so often before, warm and anxious for her mother's happiness. 'Mind you,' she said, trying to make Sarah laugh and succeeding, 'I shall be having a vile time while you're away.'

'Those two little boys – oh dear, they really are rather terrifying!'

Charlotte made a face. 'I can manage the *boys*,' she said darkly ...

As Murdo's blue car drew away from the gate, Sarah looked back and waved and waved again. Robert waved once and seemed to decide that that was quite enough. He still looked stern, but Sarah was happier for her few words with Charlotte. It was a lovely day. As they stood watching the car Nicholas and Charlotte were filled with envy. For Sarah and Robert would drive north to places with magical names – Applecross and Ullapool, Lochinver and Cape Wrath, Tongue and Altnaharra and Lairg – and it was hard to be left behind ...

The sound of the motor was suddenly taken away by the twist of the road. Silence returned. At the gate of the croft, Grahams and Latymers were held in the silence uneasily, knowing it must be broken and wondering who would speak first, who would initiate the new routine which must bind them all for the time ahead. Knowing it had better be Nicholas or Nan, Charlotte consciously held back, though it cost her something.

Nan looked at Nicholas, grimaced and shrugged.

'Now what?' she asked.

'Everybody come inside,' said Nicholas. 'We've got to make some sort of a plan. Please have your suggestions ready.'

There was something about the way he said this that changed the situation from a crisis to a challenge. As he turned for the door, the others crowded after him, all talking at once as though they had just been released from a vow of silence. They went indoors and without question or hesitation settled themselves at the table as they had done such a short time ago to hear Robert's pronouncement.

But this time it was Nicholas who took the chair with arms.

Almost without realizing what she was doing, Charlotte picked up a note pad, tore off a page for everyone and dealt them round the table.

'Have you all got pencils?'

Nobody asked what for. A flurried search began and at last they were all supplied. The meeting could begin.

Nicholas rapped on the table.

'Now then,' he said.

Everyone looked towards him expectantly. Suddenly, to his own pleased surprise, he knew that he was enjoying himself.

8 | MacBogus of Glengarble

After a little more than a week, Alison looked in the store-cupboard and wailed.

'You might think there was an army being fed. Whatever came to all the fine tins I had on the shelves?'

'We must eat,' Charlotte said.

'I suppose that makes sense. But there's never a thing left in the larder but empty holes.'

'All holes are empty,' said Roderick.

'Whisht! Did you never hear tell of a hole full of water?'

'That's a well,' Alan announced.

And before Alison could answer that, both boys removed themselves.

'They can't help answering back, Alison. It's automatic. It would be easier if there were only one of them. Or else two quite different. But they're a sort of double-boy.'

'Dear me, dear me,' said Alison, shaking her head, 'yon stepfather of yours is a powerful determined man. I thought they'd be back inside a couple of days.'

'They won't come back till they're ready,' Charlotte replied. 'Unless we asked them to. If we shouted loud enough, they'd hear all right. But I don't think there's one of us would want that. Not yet, anyway!'

'It's not the summer holiday I had in mind for you, my dearie.'

'They write wonderful letters, both of them – just as though there had never been any row and this was all part of their plans. Alison – never tell Sarah this – but since Robert was here, even those few days, I realize what Nicky and I have missed, not having a father. I never really thought of it much before.'

'Your mother managed so well all the years. She's a fine woman ... Well, mebbe I'm old-fashioned – but this seems a queer business altogether. What parents and children are about these days it's hard to see. When I heard what had happened, I near fainted away!'

'What about the MacMurdo? I don't suppose he felt particularly faint.'

'Men are strange fish. I'd best not tell you what Murdo said.'

'I can guess.' Charlotte pulled a long face and said in accents as near Murdo's as she could contrive: 'A good hiding all round'd not come amiss, forbye.'

Alison looked at her in astonishment. 'What's come to you, lass? You're the one I'd expect to be most put out by this.'

'Well, I'm not, Alison. I'm just not. I feel full of energy and determination – and being the kitchen boss is fun. The truth is, we've all been so busy getting ourselves organized we haven't had time to squabble. It's been marvellous.'

'What about Lucy?' Alison asked.

'What about her?'

'Would you say she's finding it marvellous?'

'Oh goodness, yes. Lucy's all right. I should think she's pretty well indestructible,' said Charlotte easily.

'She's young.'

'She's all right . . . Come on, let's make a shopping list. Why don't we all go to Fort William tomorrow, instead of just to Inverloch? You come, too, and we'll make a day of it. Do, Alison.'

'I'll speak to himself. He'll maybe agree.' Then Alison said again, frowning a little: 'And you're sure about Lucy?'

'Quite, quite sure, Alison.'

Lucy had turned away from the shore for once. She had noticed, half-way up the hill beyond the farm called Tigh na Garbh, an open-sided barn full of straw. That was what she needed and this was the day she meant to get it. It was a dull day, with great clouds threatening rain – the day for the job she had in mind. She was wearing her jeans and in the pockets she had an assortment of string, a pair of scissors, a large darning needle and a reel of thread, and some snippets of cotton material left over from Nan's present sewing. She had also, rolled up tight and tucked under her arm out of sight, a bright checked tablecloth which she had taken without asking from the linen cupboard.

It was no surprise to Lucy, as she turned up the track

that crossed two streams and climbed on out of sight, to discover that she was not alone. Geordie was walking behind her. She glanced over her shoulder, called 'Hi!' and then pushed on. It was nothing but a waste of time to wait for Geordie's reply, for it never came. One behind the other they plodded up the hill. It grew steeper where the track twisted in a northward direction from Kilmorah, and walking changed to scrambling.

Presently they came to the farm, and five collie dogs dashed out barking.

'Hey, fellas!' called Lucy.

The dogs skidded to a halt at the sound of a friendly voice and stood in a straggly row, grinning and waving their feathered tails.

'They could do with a tub,' Lucy said as she went on.

Beyond the farm the track ended. Here there was nothing but a path about a foot wide, the grass trampled and worn away in patches beside it. There were boulders strewn over the hillside. It was easy to imagine how the water might dash down here in winter-time.

'Nearly made it,' Lucy shouted to Geordie. 'It's a tatty old barn, too. Why don't they mend it up a little?'

From below, the barn had looked solid enough. But now she saw how dilapidated it was – no more than a handy store for winter feed.

'You should see the barn back home, Geordie. Well – I guess it's more an old stable with a loft for straw. And it's mine. It's where I do my thinking. I haven't thought much since I came to this place. A person needs somewhere quiet.'

Lucy was never sure whether Geordie was listening, or whether, if he was listening, he knew what she was talking about. Still, it was good to have someone to talk to about home, even if in this case it was rather like writing in a diary and then tearing up each page after you had come to the last line.

As they reached the barn, the rain clouds rolled low over the hilltop and bore down on them. They had to race for shelter.

'Lucky us! Come on in quick, Geordie!'

The smell of the barn was wonderful to Lucy. The straw was dry and chaffy, and she hurled herself into it and bounced with pleasure. Geordie stood watching her. She could see he was already used to her particular madness and nothing would surprise him any more. When she had got over the pleasure of being there, Lucy set about what she had come to do.

'Now you just watch this, Geordie Monroe. I'm sick of having nothing like home. So I'm going to make something.'

She began pulling a good handful of straw, choosing from the newish stack that was still firm and pliable and not likely to crumble into chaff when she touched it. She took for granted that no farmer was likely to grudge her this much of his property, though she was aware that Geordie looked cautiously back towards the farmhouse as she helped herself. She combed all the straw flat and straight with her hands, then halved it into a tidy hank. Then she made herself a place to sit in the straw, and pulled out the contents of her pockets.

Geordie sat down on the floor about a yard away from Lucy, and watched with flattering intensity as she worked – twisting and tying and snipping, and keeping up a flow of talk the entire time.

'Do you know what this is going to be? I'll say you don't. Seems like you don't have sensible things like scarecrows in Scotland – not what I call scarecrows,

anyway. Back home, two of my scarecrows are witches –
Saphira and Luciebelle – but this is a boy scarecrow.
When I've done his body I'll make him a face, and
when I've made him a face I'll make him clothes . . . Oh
jolly good!' Lucy cried in her Nicholas voice, 'I just this
minute thought what he's going to wear. A kilt! And a
plaid across his shoulder! And a bonnet on his head!'

Outside, the rain had stopped, as abruptly as it had
begun. The sun burst out with such force that all the
colours that had been hidden by the greyness of the
rain leapt out and blazed in splendour – purple heather,
red rowan berries, green mosses, blue sky, golden gorse.
Lucy was working too hard to notice. Before her eyes,
under her busy hands, the scarecrow came to life. The
comfort of home came to her and she hugged the straw
doll as though it was the most precious thing in all the
world. And yet she knew in her heart that she was not
really homesick. She had written three letters to her
grandmother by now, and all of them full of excite-

ment. The replies had been lovely to receive, but she had not watched the mail for them. There was something Lucy felt sick about, but she did not know quite what it was.

Meanwhile the straw doll was like a consolation. She had never made one herself before and he seemed to her to be quite perfect. Eyes and mouth were cut from the cotton scraps and stitched in place – and if one eye was a bit crooked, slightly lower or higher than the other one, it could be said to give character to the face. Lucy's scissors slashed through the tablecloth, then, and with pins and string she made the kilt and then the plaid, then a rather odd looking tammy – nearly bursting with satisfaction as she worked, for she had chosen exactly the right cloth for the job. With its gay lines and checks it really did look like some fantastic tartan.

'There! Look, Georgie! He's done! What'll I call him?'

She looked up to see Geordie leaving the barn. It must be his dinner time – his stomach was always their clock when they were together. How quickly the time had gone as she worked at the straw doll. She snatched up her masterpiece and ran after Geordie. He turned and looked back to see if she was following, and then dashed on – not the way they had come to the barn but in exactly the opposite direction.

It only took Lucy a second to realize that since they had come in a kind of spiral up the hillside to the barn, there must be a short cut over the summit – and that was the way Geordie was going.

This way there was no path at all. Geordie led Lucy over mounds of boulders where the tough-growing whins scratched her ankles as she jumped down again to ground level. He took her through beds of thick heather where she walked as though on springs. Ahead of her, he scrambled and leapt, and she followed. Quite suddenly they were at the highest point and looking down towards the shore. There was the sea, there the reefs, there the dunes. They were high above the scattered crofts – their own two homes, and the Johnstones', from which just then Alison emerged to peg a load of washing on the line.

Geordie knelt on a great flat outcropping of stone that was like a plate set at the summit of the hill. He looked about him in obvious pleasure. Catching colour from the sky, that was dazzling now between great clouds, the burn flowed down the hillside below. It looked like a steel ribbon running to the base of the high hill, then twisting to run along beside Geordie's home and under the little bridge at the gate. At last, beyond Alison's hedge and wall, it dropped sharply over stones, then fanned out where the sands began and vanished.

'It's like a map,' Lucy cried. 'I never saw the ocean that blue before. No – it isn't blue at all – it's purple. It's purple like a plum. Wouldn't you say it was like a plum, Geordie?'

She did not, naturally, expect a reply; she had always to *look* for Geordie's answers. So now she looked towards the great jutting rock to see how he felt about the ocean looking like a plum – but he was no longer there.

Lucy stared around her in bewilderment – then, very quickly and sharply, in alarm. Home was in sight, truly, but how far below. Up there, high above roofs and shore, she might have been in another world, a world full of Highland mystery and magic that could surely hold her as and how it chose.

'Geordie! Geordie, come on and stop fooling! Think I don't know you're hiding? Geordie! Geordie Monroe!'

At first there was no sound at all. Then she heard his shrill whistle. But she couldn't see him anywhere. The whistle came again. It was directly below her. She lay flat on the rock and looked downwards. There he was – half-way down, leaping from rock to rock where the burn flowed in the beginnings of a fall, pausing only a second at a time to put his fingers in his mouth and whistle up at her.

Lucy lay on the rock and considered the situation. She was much too high up for her liking. Her heart was pumping unpleasantly. She was afraid she felt a little sick. Geordie looked tiny. How could he have left her without help? But he was obviously enjoying himself. Indeed there was little doubt he had brought her this way to show her and share with her something of his own. If he could go home that way, so surely could she. True, he was a genuine Highland laddie and knew the ways of his own countryside – but wasn't she a Graham? It would have been just too easy to turn round and go back the way they had come. But Lucy felt there was a challenge here. She knew she must follow Geordie.

'*Wait*, can't you?'

She eased herself back from the rock and looked about her for the start of his way down. Then she saw it, looking almost like a flight of stone steps, only with a very good distance between each tread. At least at this time of year the water ran round the stones and not over them, as it must do in winter. What a great thundering torrent it would be then – it made Lucy shiver to think of it.

She clutched the scarecrow under her left arm and jumped. For a second she thought she would over-balance, but her foot was firm enough. She took the next leap down and then the next. It was so unexpectedly easy that she could understand why Geordie had gone down fast – she would want to come here again herself – it was exciting once you knew how . . .

At the fifth boulder Lucy slipped a bit, grabbed at a bush that held her kindly – and dropped the scarecrow.

She saw it falling, turning head over heels – over and over and over – and thought that could surely happen to her, too. She was filled with a terrible panic. She thought she heard herself scream. She grabbed the bush with both hands and as she did so she began to slither.

She looked down, not down the steep slope to where Geordie was, but down between her own two feet. The bush was growing out of a fissure in the rock. She saw it, a black slit like a wickedly open mouth waiting to swallow her.

The bush, giving to her weight, began to bend outwards. Lucy tried to heave herself back on to the stone, and if she had done so and recovered her balance, she could still have continued on her way. But the falling straw doll had made her dizzy. She was very frightened. She might have been the last person in all the world, hanging on to a bush on a mountain side, and knowing that something was sure to give in a second or two.

She screamed out: 'Geordie! Help!' And before she could know if he had heard her, the bush bent farther and farther from safety, and she began to fall . . .

It was just before one o'clock. The rain had gone over now and the sun was brilliant. Charlotte had stayed at home to get ready the picnic lunch which she would then take down to the shore. They had a regular rendezvous there. Anyone could do as he wanted all the morning, but there at the appointed spot the food would be at one o'clock, and whoever failed to arrive could go hungry. One of the most interesting things about life as lived without parents was that it all turned out to be much stricter. They had masses of rules. They kept making new ones and writing them down, and there was absolutely no sympathy for anyone who broke them. Who could imagine Sarah letting any of them go without food because of unpunctuality? But once when Alan and Roderick had not turned up until supper was cleared away and washed up even Nan had agreed that they could go hungry to bed. And once, when they were going to Inverloch by car, Charlotte could not decide what to wear and kept everybody waiting – until at last Nicholas had made Murdo drive off without her. It was all pretty tough – but it was fair.

Charlotte gathered up the packets of sandwiches, the cake Alison had baked them, the apples and the biscuits and the orange juice, and packed them all into two baskets. She was at the door when Alan and Roderick appeared. They were wearing bathing trunks with their shirts over them and they looked exaggeratedly long-legged and thin.

'Are you hungry?' Charlotte asked. 'I'm just coming.'

'Sure we're hungry,' agreed Alan. 'We're always hungry.'

'But guess what,' said Roderick. 'We've come to carry the baskets.'

'Are you *that* hungry?' cried Charlotte – aware that she had fallen into the language Nan called Yankish.

'Yes, we are. But guess again. Just today, Nick made a new rule. No baggage-carrying by females.'

Charlotte smiled and handed over the baskets. Most of all she was pleased by that *Nick*. It had been some time before Alan and Roderick had found themselves able to call Nicholas anything but *you* or *him* ...

'You'll never stop Lucy carrying her own things.'

'Oh Lucy – she may be a female but she's her own boss,' said Alan.

'Where is she, anyway?' asked Roderick.

'Hasn't she been with you?'

'Haven't seen her all morning. Nan said she'd surely be with you and the food.'

Charlotte frowned. 'Where's she got to, I wonder? Oh well – she'll turn up for lunch.'

'Guess she will – or else she's up to something.'

'Yes, sir – you never can tell with Lucy what she's thinking of doing next.'

This was quite the longest conversation Charlotte had had with Alan and Roderick. She felt as pleased as if two sharp little animals, with an inclination to bite, had decided instead to accept sugar from her fingers. She went out of the gate and along the track with one boy on either side of her, each carrying a basket.

'What's gotten into Geordie?' Alan said suddenly. 'Will you listen to that? He can *talk*!'

Geordie was racing towards them, his face bright red, his mouth opening and closing in the most unusual fashion as he bellowed:

'It's yon Lucy! It's yon Lucy!'

'What's happened?' cried Charlotte. 'Geordie! What is it? Where's Lucy?'

'She's fell in a great hole and likely broke her neck!'

'Geordie!'

'Will I take you where she's lying?'

Geordie seemed to choose all the most dramatic and appalling words with which to break his silence.

'Quick!' Charlotte cried.

Geordie began to run back the way he had come and Charlotte ran with him, shouting to the boys as she went:

'Get Nicky! Get Nan! Find a rope!'

She did not stop to consider how they would follow if she disappeared after Geordie, but they dealt with that.

'I'll stay by the bridge and keep them in sight,' Alan said. 'You go get the others.'

Roderick dashed off. Alan ran at a jog trot to the bridge over the burn. He watched Geordie lead Charlotte across the rough ground at the foot of the steep hillside, and then start upward, using the bed of the stream as a track...

'Is it far?' Charlotte asked, panting, as she struggled and scrambled after Geordie.

'Aye, it's a wee step.'

'Did you – what happened...?' But Charlotte gave that up. She had not enough breath to talk and climb, he was clearly taking her to the place as fast as he possibly could, and whatever might have happened she would certainly discover when she got there. Geordie's lugubrious talk of broken necks she put firmly out of her mind. Then she cried out: 'Oh, what's that?'

For a second she thought she was looking at Lucy herself, lying by the side of the burn as it dropped down the hillside.

'Yon's her straw dolly,' said Geordie. 'She dropped it, you ken. It was the last thing she did.'

Charlotte gave him a quick and venomous look but said nothing. She looked above her. Surely they were nearly at the top? No wonder the locals called this hill a mountain. The silence was terrifying. It seemed as though Lucy could only be lying injured and unconscious...

Then she heard a voice, crying half in fright and misery, half in extreme anger:

'Oh come on somebody – come save my life, quick! Oh why won't someone come? Geordie – you said you'd go fetch help! Geordie! Anyone! Come and help me!'

'Lucy! Coming! Lucy – it's all right!'

'Oh ... Oh gee ...' The voice tailed away.

'She's fast down yon wee crack,' said Geordie. 'She'll likely stay there till she dies ...'

'Oh shut up, do,' snapped Charlotte. And even at that moment she knew that having once shut him up she would never get him to speak again – he would be back in his own peculiar silence from now on. She hauled herself up on to the edge of the fissure. It was not so very difficult. Indeed only the meanest chance had dropped Lucy on the very spot where there was a hole instead of good heathery hillside.

Charlotte peered into the gloom.

'Sarah!' cried Lucy wildly.

'It's Charlotte. Are you hurt?'

Lucy's voice changed instantly:

'I should think I'm just about dead! I'm hitched up on this old bush and my pants are torn and I'm miserable!'

Charlotte was so relieved to find nothing worse that she grinned down at Lucy.

'I think you're as brave as a lion – I really do. If I were down there I'd be sobbing with fright.'

'I've *done* that. Get me out!'

'Can you reach my hand?'

'I can reach. But that way we'll both pull our arms right off.'

She was about right. Already Charlotte could hear

the sleeve of her shirt ripping – her favourite butter-yellow shirt. She shifted back a bit and tried to see how she might redeploy herself to pull Lucy to safety. Then she heard shouts below and looking down she saw Nan and the three boys, complete with a coil of rope, clambering up to join them.

Nan shouted: 'Is she okay?'

'She's wild with rage,' Charlotte called back. 'Hurry with the rope. I can't get at her.'

Nicholas and Nan reached Charlotte's side. They peered in their turn at Lucy, who suddenly broke into cackling laughter at the row of heads against the sky.

'I don't believe she's even going to apologize,' said Nicholas.

'Wait'll I get at her,' cried Nan.

But she was shivering with sheer reaction at finding Lucy more or less safe. Charlotte felt the shivering and she pulled Nan to one side and made her sit down.

'We don't want you falling in after her.'

'Ran too fast up the hill, I guess,' said Nan. 'Oh Charlotte, honey – your lovely shirt's all *mangled*!'

Nicholas was giving orders. 'Hang on to this, Alan. Look out – it's just too easy to slip down this slope. It's steep as a wall. Lucy – you're going to get scratched to bits when we start hauling. Can you put something over your face? Have you got a hanky?'

'Do I ever? I'll just shut my eyes and wish. Okay, brother – pull!'

So with much heaving and hauling, squealing from Lucy, shouts of advice from the rest and black silence from Geordie, they got Lucy out of the hole and sat her on a rock to recover. Charlotte hugged Lucy, but Lucy did not hug Charlotte back. And Nan did not hug Lucy at all – in fact she was quite tough with her little sister.

Not a bad thing, Charlotte decided. She had felt sadly rebuffed when Lucy pushed her away. But she also recalled a curious fact. At the moment when Lucy had realized help had arrived, it was not Nan or Charlotte or any one of them she had wanted to see, but Sarah.

'Here's your old scarecrow,' Alan said, pushing it at Lucy. 'For pete's sake – where'd that come from?'

'I made it. So what?'

'I should think you did make it,' Charlotte said. 'That's one of our favourite tableclothes. Lucy!'

Nicholas took the straw doll from Lucy. Its fall had sent its bonnet over the one straight eye, leaving a general appearance of such lopsidedness that it was difficult to look at the creature without bursting into laughter.

'Bless me,' said Nicholas, shaking his head. 'See who it is, Charley?' He flipped at the kilt and the plaid made from the tablecloth.

'Well, I'm not sure . . . Unless . . . Is it . . .?'

'Gimme,' said Lucy rudely, snatching back the doll.

'Treat him respectfully, please,' said Nicholas, frowning. 'I'd have you know this is a Highland notability, Lucy my dear. This is none other than the MacBogus, Chief of Clan Glengarble.'

Lucy stared at Nicholas, and then at the doll. For all her bravado she had been looking very white. Now colour came back into her face and her eyes sparkled.

'It is?' she said. 'Are you sure?'

'I'm certain.'

'Well – what d'you know?' said Lucy, very satisfied indeed. She looked beaming round at the rest. 'Come on, then – what are you all waiting for? Let's get on down. I'm hungry!'

9 | The Laird

Nan tidied up the MacBogus that same evening. She stitched his kilt and hemmed his plaid and put his bonnet to rights. Charlotte moaned a bit about the tablecloth, but not too much.

'He needs a feather to his bonnet,' Lucy said, sounding like Alison.

'Hoots,' cried Alan, 'he'll be needing three. He's chief of all the Clan Glengarble, Nick said.'

There was a collection of seagull's feathers stuck in a jar above the fireplace. Lucy looked at them hopefully.

'Oh all right,' Nicholas said, sighing exaggeratedly. 'A chap can't even keep his feather collection in peace.'

'Thanks, Nicky.' Lucy grabbed the jar. Perhaps the

feathers should really have been eagles' feathers, but these would do.

Since the experience of the morning, Lucy seemed more herself than she had done for days. Almost cock-a-hoop, Nicholas had told her. And he had added privately in her ear: 'That's twice you've had to be rescued. Keep the third time at bay, will you please, dear Lucy?' She didn't like him when he spoke in that extra-English play-acting voice, so she did not answer. He was the only one who sounded a note of rebuke. The others, even Nan, made a fuss of her – which was nice. Indeed, that was a very mellow evening they spent. The rain had returned, it beat about the cottage walls but they were snug inside with a fire burning in the big grate. Murdo had brought them six fat trout caught by Euan that afternoon in the loch, and Charlotte cooked them with – as Nan said – 'drawn butter and lemon wedges'. Three girls, three boys and the MacBogus crowded round the table. There was not a frown to be seen, not a cross word to be heard. Nobody knew how it had happened or even paused to wonder. It had just happened and it was perfect.

'This is the best cooking Charley has ever cooked,' Nicholas said, as the last bone was picked.

'Is it?' Charlotte looked round the table. 'What do you think, Nan? The butter's the least bit salt. And I'm sure I should have used black pepper.'

'Honey, it's just wonderful. Do you have the recipe?'

'You just *must* call it *receipt* in Scotland, Nan.'

'Well, okay I will. Do you have the receipt?'

'*Have* you the receipt, lassie?' corrected Nicholas.

'Either way, it needs black pepper,' Charlotte said.

But Nicholas waved away these scruples of an anxious cook.

'I'll wager there's no better meal been served in Scotland's length and breadth the night,' he declaimed. 'No, not even in the grandest hotel in all the land, where the Graham dines with his lady.'

'Oh Nicky!' Charlotte almost bounced in her chair. 'How wonderful it sounds!'

'Like he's the chief,' cried Lucy. 'That's what it means, I guess, when you call Daddy the Graham.'

'Yes,' Nicholas decided, 'that *is* what it means, Lucy.' He suddenly jumped up in a very excited fashion. 'Tell you what – we'll drink their health. Quick, Nan – there's some more Coke in the kitchen – and some ginger beer. Quick – get it open! Get it open! Get it open!'

Everyone sprang up and started dashing about in a wild way, yelling instructions about bottles and bottle-openers and glasses. At last they were all back in their places, their glasses were filled and they stood looking to Nicholas, who had leapt up on his chair and put one foot on the table in what seemed a very Highland fashion. He raised his glass high.

'Ladies and Gentleman and Others,' he cried. 'I give you a toast. I give you health and prosperity and great contentment to the Graham and Mistress Sarah of that Ilk.'

'For crying out loud – what's an ilk?'

'Never mind that now. Are you all ready to drink? Shout it out then –'

'The Graham and Mistress Sarah and the Ilk!' shouted Lucy wildly above all the rest.

'Drink up and no heel taps!'

'Ilks and heel taps! It's a foreign language!'

'Drink, you scum!' bawled Nicholas.

Glasses were clashed dangerously together again and

again. It seemed an awful lot to drink off at one go, but Nicholas kept shouting that not a drop – he was careful to say *drap* – must be left in any glass. So on they went, gulping and spluttering as laughter got the better of them, the ginger beer nearly making them sneeze, until at last there was no dreg left.

'Let me see them! Hold your glasses upside down!'

Everyone held out his glass over the table and not the smallest drip fell on to the cloth.

'We ought to smash them!' Charlotte cried.

'Smash them? The glasses?'

'Yes, of course. That's what you're supposed to do with a loyal toast – smash the glasses so that they can never be used again – then the toast can never be sullied.'

'Wait a minute –' Nicholas protested.

'It's no good waiting. That'll spoil it.'

'I'm sure you only do it when you drink a *loyal* toast – to the Queen or someone.'

'Well this is someone, isn't it? *And* it's loyal. It's the Graham – it's the Laird!'

'The Laird!' Nicholas looked at his sister and just for a second it was as if they were alone in the room. 'Charley – that's what we've been waiting for. Now we know what to call him.'

'The Laird. Yes. I said nicknames just have to happen.'

'All right,' Nicholas cried to all the rest. 'Break your glasses! Hurl them into the fire!' And shouting: 'The Laird! The Laird!' he threw his own glass hard and it shivered against the iron edge of the fender.

For a fraction of a second the rest hesitated. Then Lucy shouted – and threw. Then Alan – Roderick – Charlotte – Nan ... Within seconds they stood looking down at a welter of glass, bits and chips and splinters lying in the hearth and on the rug before it, glinting and glittering as feverishly as was fitting for an occasion so charged with magnificent drama.

'Oh gosh,' said Charlotte then, recovering her breath. 'Now we'll have to clear it all up . . .'

Even the discovery that two of Sarah's favourite glasses had been among those sacrificed could not really spoil the splendour of that moment. It had been something huge and impulsive and full of meaning. Sarah would understand. She would be the first to consider two glasses, even favourite ones, a small price to pay for the result. It was the first time they had all obeyed an identical impulse – the first time they had all been part of one another. Nothing would ever be the same again – and the excellence of that was that it could only be better.

Murdo had agreed to drive them to the town the following day. Alison was to go, too. When they had all climbed in the brake was packed tight, and as everybody had shopping to do it was going to be packed even tighter on the return trip. They were all extremely cheerful. That morning there had been a letter from Sarah. It had been addressed to Nicholas. But without pause, he had ripped open the envelope, unfolded the page and read it aloud to all the rest. That had made a good start to the day.

'What's come to you?' Alison asked, looking from one to another. 'Every one of you's a dog with two tails.'

'We're just mighty glad it's a fine day,' said Lucy.

'Let's hope it'll be fine a week the day. It's the school outing, and it's been talked of a twelvemonth already.'

'Is Geordie going?'

'I haven't a doubt of it – though it's little use to ask him. You might go along with them if you pleased, Lucy. There's always a place or two going begging.'

'I wouldn't know even one soul there. There'd only be Geordie to talk to – and that gets to be like talking in your sleep.'

'Ah well – you could always change your mind. Miss MacDougal's in charge – she'd look after you.'

Nan was next to Murdo in the front seat, then Nicholas.

'I'll have to practise driving right-handed,' Nan said. 'I could take a turn on the way home – couldn't I?'

'Indeed you could not,' replied Murdo, shocked. 'You're not old enough to drive a vehicle of any sort whatsoever.'

Nan laughed. 'But I have my own car back home!'

'Will you listen to that, Alison?' cried Murdo. 'And she still in school.'

Nicholas said: 'Nan, you're shooting a line.'

'There's plenty of high-school kids with cars,' cried Roderick.

'But she's not old enough –'

'I am, too. I'm sixteen years and six months, and by then anyone can drive in the U.S.A. Daddy gave me a car on my birthday. And if you all don't want to believe me, I guess it's written down somewhere that number U 35.409 is the property of Miss Nicole Ann Graham.'

'Miss *Who*?'

'Didn't you know? Her name's not really Nan at all,' said Lucy. 'Nicole Ann's just too much of a mouthful.'

Nicholas was silent a moment. He frowned at Nan.

'You're a dark horse, my girl,' he said at last.

'Nan's a horse and Sarah's an ilk,' remarked Lucy.

'What's the child got into her mind now?'

'What's an ilk, then, Alison?'

'There's no such thing. It's just a word meaning *the same*.'

'The same as a *horse*?'

'I give up,' said Alison. 'Murdo Johnstone, you're driving too fast for my liking.'

Nicholas was still frowning at Nan.

'When's your birthday, then?' he demanded.

'November tenth. It's the first party after Hallowe'en.'

Charlotte cried in astonishment: 'Then goodness – you're practically twins. His birthday's the ninth!'

'Oh I think that's just wonderful!' Lucy cried. 'You can have a double party. Twice everything!'

'Nothing of the sort, I'm afraid,' replied Nicholas. 'It just can't happen. When November comes Nan will be "in high school" in Massachusetts, and I shall be at Clere Combe.'

A strange little silence fell on this pronouncement. It was the first time any of them had ever said a word about the end of the holidays and their parting. The weeks ahead had seemed endless, but they were going over already. It was not easy for any of them to know what they felt about this. A week ago – perhaps even yesterday – they would have been sure to say at once that it would be a very good thing when the holidays ended and they were no longer expected to behave like brothers and sisters.

'I guess Granny misses us,' Lucy said thoughtfully.

In spite of this interlude, or perhaps even because of it, the day at Fort William was a success. Murdo went off about his own affairs, Charlotte and Nan and Alison set about the household shopping, while Nicholas took

Lucy and the two boys to make their own particular purchases. When the stores were all bought and had been stowed in the car, there were still things to be done. Alison needed knitting wool, Nan wanted some material for sewing, Charlotte had to buy a cotton shirt to replace the one she had torn during Lucy's dramatic rescue.

Charlotte and Nan stood in a draper's shop, looking at materials, wondering which to choose.

'This is where I got the stuff for your bedroom curtains,' Charlotte said.

'You did? You mean – they're new?'

'Alison made them up.'

Nan said nothing for a moment. She looked at Charlotte with her head a little bent and her hair falling over one cheek in a very characteristic way. Charlotte felt herself turning rather red. She had not meant to tell Nan that the curtains had been chosen and made specially for her and Lucy.

'Look, honey,' said Nan. 'I have a swell idea. Why not let me make you a new shirt? I know just exactly how. I only need your measurements.'

Charlotte's flush then was one of pleasure.

'Would you? Would you really? I think that would be wonderful, Nan – because just look at that marvellous red stuff. It's exactly what I like but I'll never, never find a ready-made shirt that colour.'

'Okay, then. It's the red. Come on! What are we waiting for?'

The day went on as it had begun, amiably and easily. They bought sandwiches and buns and fruit and ate a very late lunch by the side of the loch. After yesterday's rain everything was clean and clear. Under the water you could see rock and weed and sometimes small darting fish. The sky was cloudless, except for a tumble of white along the far horizon.

'There's a change coming,' said Murdo.

'Oh Murdo, how can there be? It looks set fair for weeks.'

'You might think so, without the eye to see,' he replied. He looked reprovingly at the doubting Charlotte. 'It takes many good years of a man's life to get to telling the weather. You've a sharp tongue for your own opinion, lass, but you cannot have an eye for the

weather at your tender age. It would not be reasonable at all.'

'Bet you sixpence!' cried Charlotte.

'Sixpence! Losh, woman, there's a way to waste good siller! Your aunt, now – she'd an eye for the weather as wise as any in the Highlands. She was a grand woman ... I mind a day, and it was just such a day as this one, when she stood me out there'd be a gale before the week was through. Sure enough – the wind blew from the south-west for days at gale force. And there was great destruction – great destruction.'

They were sitting in a row on a low wall near the water, and Murdo was somewhere in the middle of them all. As he spoke, they all grew silent, and to right and left of him they leant forward to listen and to watch his serious face.

'What happened?' asked Lucy.

'Great trees fell like faggots. A hundred boats at a time were smashed on the shores. And the face of the loch was whipped into towers of water.'

'Christmas!' muttered Alan.

'How awful, Murdo,' Nan said, in her soft voice. 'What did you do when it was past?'

'We cleared up the mess in the customary fashion,' replied Murdo. 'A natural disaster's no such a bad thing once in a while.'

'Will you listen to him?' Alison rolled up her eyes. 'Away with you, Murdo Johnstone. It's a fine day the day and we want no talk of natural disasters.'

'No, indeed,' agreed Nicholas. 'After all, we've got Lucy.'

Lucy hurled herself at him, shrieking her protests. Nicholas picked her up easily and swung her towards the water. But it was too like the moment when he had upended Alan, that dreadful day at Ardtorquil. So he set her down quickly.

'One doughnut left!' he cried. 'Whose?'

'Mine!' Lucy grabbed it and raced off, and Nicholas raced after her. Alan and Roderick shouted encouragements, but it was difficult to know whose side they were on.

'Do those two *always* agree?' Charlotte asked Nan.

'They've been like that ever since Mommy was killed. They just got close in together. I guess that's the way

they need to be, whether we like it, or whether we
don't.'

Charlotte wanted to say something to Nan that would
sound helpful and wise and understanding. But she
could not find the right words at all.

It was Nan who offered her wisdom, and courage,
too.

'Things just happen,' she said, smiling a little. 'They
just happen, honey, and there's nothing anyone can
do.'

As they drove home that afternoon, it was hard to
believe that the weather was likely to break. It was
hardest of all for the Grahams, unaccustomed to the
quick and dramatic changes of Scottish weather. They
had had more than their share of sunshine already,
whether they realized it or not.

When they reached Kilmorah and the cluster of
buildings near the quay, Euan came out of the post
office with a letter. He stood in the road and waved the
letter like a flag, and the car stopped.

'Who's it for, Euan?' Nicholas shouted.

'It's for Miss Graham,' replied Euan, coming to the
side of the car and handing the letter to Nan with a
bow.

'Oh,' said Nan. 'Thanks. I don't get called Miss
Graham much in Winterfield, Mass.' Then she looked
at the envelope. 'Guess who?' she cried. 'It's from the
Laird. Let's read it right away.'

It was Euan who suggested a day's fishing. Murdo
willingly fell in with the idea. There were to be two
boats and they planned to fish the loch to the east. Euan
had suggested sea fishing, really, but Murdo declined
this. Although forty-eight hours had passed since he

had prophesied a change in the weather, and although absolutely nothing had happened, he still maintained the break would come. He did not intend to be caught off-shore in a squall – with a load, as he said, of other people's children.

The plan meant an early start. Charlotte was downstairs before six o'clock, getting breakfast ready and seeing about a packed lunch.

Nan was down early, too, but instead of going at once to help Charlotte in the kitchen, she went into the living-room. There Alison's sewing-machine was set up on one end of the table, surrounded by pieces of red cotton material, reels of thread, pins, scissors, tape measure, thimble. Nan picked up her work and looked at it anxiously. She had not wanted to admit when she went to bed the previous night that something had gone wrong with the scarlet shirt she was making for Charlotte. During the night, she hoped, some magic would have taken place and everything would have become quite straightforward again. But there had been no magic after all. The sewing had gone wrong and there was no point in denying it. But Nan did not want, yet, to admit this to Charlotte.

Nan went into the kitchen.

'Hi!'

'Hi!' replied Charlotte.

'What'll I do to help?'

'Could you put filling in these sandwiches? Honestly, if I see many more sandwiches I shall start having nightmares. I've cut hunky ones, look, then there needn't be so many. There's ham and stuff in the larder. Put in a lot. It's easier.'

Nan set about doing as she was told. Charlotte talked all the time she worked, but Nan was very quiet.

'Look, honey,' she said at last, 'I guess I'll stay home today. I'm not all that crazy about fishing.'

'Oh Nan – it'll be lovely. Not the fishing – I don't care much about that, either – but being out on the loch.'

'I'd sooner stay home. Honest.'

'All by yourself? That seems pretty miserable and we shan't be back for ages and ages.'

'Well, that's how it's got to be. Sorry.'

'Well – okay, then,' said Charlotte reluctantly. She sounded disappointed. She was disappointed.

When the time came, Nan watched the rest set out. Charlotte, Alan and Roderick were to go with Murdo in his boat; Nicholas and Lucy with Euan – plus Geordie who had come grinning with pleasure to take Nan's place. Euan had gone on ahead to get the boats and tackle ready, so the rest piled uncomfortably into Murdo's bright blue car and off they went.

As soon as she was alone, Nan went and got her sewing. She hurried to the bedroom she shared with Lucy and tried the bright shirt on herself. It was a wonderful colour – full and sharp as a poppy. The back and the two fronts seemed all right. It was the sleeves that had gone wrong. They pulled and dragged, made the collar poke out at the back of the neck and the front fastenings look all crooked.

'The whole thing's just *awful*,' Nan said in misery. 'What'll I do now?'

There was nothing for it but to start unpicking. When she had undone both armholes Nan realized her mistake. She had cut two left sleeves. The material was slightly different on its right side, so there was no way of getting out of the difficulty save by cutting a new sleeve. And she had used up all the material.

Nan sat down and cried. It was not only that she hated the thing having gone wrong – it was not that she felt she had taken on more than she was capable of, that she looked a bit of a fool and Charlotte would still be shirtless. It was because she had genuinely wanted to do something for Charlotte. The moment Nicholas had called Robert *the Laird* something had happened to Nan – and it must have happened to the others, too, though they might not have been aware of it in quite the same way. Nan had immediately felt herself a part of something established and comfortable – something she could not have explained in words. It was as though she and Lucy and the boys, and Nicholas and Charlotte, were all pieces of a puzzle that had seemed impossible to fit together – and then quite suddenly they had all begun to slip into place. This was not a thing that could be spoken out loud. To make Charlotte the red shirt that she so much wanted had seemed to Nan one little impulsive way of expressing it.

And now it had all gone wrong. The tears poured down Nan's cheeks. She was not greatly given to crying, but once she started she found it hard to stop. What could she do? What *could* she do to put things right and not have her gesture ruined by the stupid lack of a small length of cotton material?

There was only one remedy – to buy some more. Her tears stopped abruptly. She looked at the clock. Barely nine. It was seventy miles to the town but far less if you used the ferry. With any luck she could be there and back before the others returned from fishing. And then no one need ever know that she had helped herself to the car.

Very rapidly, Nan began getting rid of the tear stains and preparing herself for the journey to Fort William.

Within fifteen minutes she was in the garage inspecting the car. Although she had never handled a right-hand drive before, as she had said to Murdo, it would surely not take her long to get used to it. Fortunately, the key was hanging in the dashboard. With her heart beating faster than was comfortable, Nan settled herself and pressed the starter. The engine obligingly kicked instantly, turned over and settled to an eager throbbing.

'We're off!' murmured Nan.

She threw in the clutch and reversed out of the garage, turned neatly on the sandy track and set her nose towards Kilmorah and the long narrow road to the town.

10 | One Step Forward, Two Steps Back

It was wonderful to be driving again. One of the hardest things for Nan about this vacation had been leaving her own little car behind. She had not believed it at first, when her father told her she would not be able to drive in England or Scotland until she was seventeen and had passed a stiff test. He had also asked her not to say too much about owning her car. She had realized why, of course; it would be dreadfully galling for Nicholas, and she knew her father was right to be so tactful about the business. She had not meant to speak of it ever, and when it slipped out on the way to Fort William with Murdo she had regretted it.

There was not too much traffic on the winding one-track road. The fine weather took people early to the waterside, and on the shores of the lochs and the Sound and farther round the coast, they settled in for the whole day. As she drove on the stretch high above the

142

loch, Nan looked down at the broad blue water and tried to decide which of many small boats might be Murdo's and which Euan's. But it was impossible to tell. Once she stopped the car and stared hard because she really thought she had spotted them. But the water was slightly ruffled, the boats bobbed inconveniently, so that she could not even count the number of people in each. Besides, more interesting than the boats, Nan found, were the herons fishing along the shore, rising lazily on their huge strong wings, beating a few yards farther down-current, then settling again.

It was much easier driving on what seemed to her the wrong side than Nan would have expected. In no time at all she had stopped groping for her gears with her right hand and settled happily to the new rhythm. After a time, she began to sing to the car, just as if it were her own that she loved so dearly. She forbade herself any further distractions, she had wasted too much time looking at boats and herons. Whatever happened, she must contrive to get home ahead of the others and this was no way to set about it. She knew all too well what Nicholas would say – and what he would feel – if he discovered she had taken the car out. And of course he was perfectly right. Apart from any outrage to his personal feelings, there was the little fact that she was breaking the law. If anyone caught her it might be just too terrible. Might they even lock her up?

The trouble was that because the law she was breaking belonged to a country other than her own, Nan simply could not take this part of the business at all seriously. She felt only that as she was an American citizen allowances must be made in a country where the same language – more or less – was spoken.

'Wonder if I'm going to need gas,' Nan said to herself. But the tank was three-quarters full. So she put words to her wordless song, chanting as she went: *'Plenty of gas in the tank, In the tank there is plenty of gas. I figured the tank would be empty, That it might not have gas – But it has.* And a good thing, too,' she added, 'because it looks like I don't have enough money to take the ferry – and that means driving the whole way round the darn loch.'

In spite of this, Nan reached Fort William in good time. She had no difficulty with the traffic. She parked the car outside the Museum and went to buy the red material. As she walked into the shop she had a sudden horrible fear that the whole lot might have been sold during the two days since she had bought the first length. But there was nothing to worry about. She made her purchase and left the shop. Feeling extremely satisfied with her own efficiency, Nan started her homeward drive at precisely one o'clock. Unless she was delayed in some way, or unless the fishing party broke up long before it was intended to, she could hardly fail to be safely home before the others.

In fact, she soon found herself making slower progress on the return journey. The morning's breeze at her back had become a stiffish south-west wind and the car was buffeted uncomfortably. She was checked from the moment she turned along the lochside and immediately began losing time. She made it up on the stretch across the glen, driving faster than she had done yet, loving the feel of the car, even though it was so much heavier to handle than her own.

But now she found the traffic had increased. There was a long stretch with several villages to pass through. The change in the weather was bringing people back from their waterside amusements to their various hotels and lodgings. It was constantly necessary to pull into a passing place to let oncoming traffic through – equally she had herself to wait while other drivers moved out of her path.

Within ten miles of Kilmorah the road conditions improved, for the traffic always thinned on this stretch – unless you had business in Kilmorah there was nowhere else the road could take you. Unfortunately, a lorry ahead of Nan had business in Kilmorah and the driver saw no reason for letting her past. Although she hooted – quite gently and politely – there was no sign that the driver intended to pull off the road for her, which was the only way she could overtake him. After a bit, Nan saw the grinning face of the driver reflected in his own long-armed mirror and realized that he was amusing himself. There was nothing to do but endure the delay. She trailed along behind him, trying to look dignified.

At last a second car came up behind Nan and hooted impatiently. Surprisingly the lorry driver then obliged. At the next scoop he pulled smartly off the road. Nan put her foot down and rushed onward, with the following car pressing up behind.

By now she was late. She began to drive really fast. The car behind seemed as keen to pass her as she had been keen to pass the truck, but Nan was determined to keep ahead. The car behind her hooted several times, and once flashed its lights at her. That settled it. Nothing would induce her to let by so ill-tempered a driver. It was ridiculous to pretend she was holding him up as she herself had been held up by the slow-going lorry.

Nan drove faster and faster on the narrow road. The driver of an oncoming car, pulling hastily into a scoop to let her by, shouted at her as she passed. She had no idea what he said, but she shouted back. She knew she was behaving like an idiot but somehow she could not stop.

At last the car behind gave such a violent blast that Nan gave in. There was a passing place on the side of the hill that led on to the last stretch before Kilmorah. Nan pulled in there and impatiently waved on the following car.

It stopped ahead of her, however. Two men got out. Policemen.

'Yon's no decent way for a young lady like yourself to be driving a narrow road,' said the first policeman, standing beside the car and looking down at her. He was tall and broad and solemn. 'You've no wish, I take it, to be killing yourself or any other traveller in these parts?'

'I'm sorry,' Nan said, looking up at him as she sat helplessly at the wheel. 'I guess I was hurrying.'

'I guess that was clear to the meanest intelligence,' he replied.

'You wouldn't give me a ticket, though, would you?' Nan said, trying to smile at him.

'A ticket?'

The younger policeman butted in: 'That's American for a summons, Angus.'

'Aye. I recognize the language, forbye. Have you your licence with you?'

Nan shook her head.

'It's at home, maybe?'

'I don't have one. I'm only on vacation here. I'm an American citizen and I just don't have a British licence.'

'She would not be needing one, Angus,' said the young policeman.

'I have that in mind. But I'd be glad to hear you address me as Sergeant, Constable.'

'I have my own automobile back home,' Nan broke in desperately.

'Indeed? Indeed, have you? And that means you are – how old would it be?'

Nan bit her lip. 'Seventeen in November.'

'That's too late by months, you ken. You cannot drive a motor car in any part of the United Kingdom before you are seventeen years of age.'

'Oh gee, that's tough,' said Nan miserably. 'That sure is tough for any American.'

'It is tough only for Americans under seventeen,' replied Sergeant Angus, 'and they are the ones who matter just now. I will see you to your home. Move over now – into the passenger seat.'

'You mean – you're going to drive me home?'

'That is my intention. This is Mistress Latymer's car, is it not?'

'She's Mrs Graham now. She's my stepmother,' said Nan, slightly astounded at hearing herself claim Sarah in this fashion. 'She'll be mad. She'll be mad at me. You must know how stepmothers are . . .'

But she was not Nicholas, who could act a part, no doubt even to a policeman.

'Whisht, lassie,' said the sergeant, in a suddenly fatherly fashion, 'I am well acquainted with the good lady.'

Miserably, Nan slid over into the passenger seat. The sergeant took the wheel. Driven by one policeman, with the second bringing up the rear as though to cut off any escape, Nan returned to Kilmorah.

Once things had started to go wrong, they seemed to slide and slide into a positive abyss. Nan was suddenly aware that on either side of the car as it took the last hill towards the croft, a small boy was running.

'That's my sister!' yelled Alan.

'Hi, Nan – what's cooking?' shouted Roderick.

What in the world were they doing back so soon? Nan looked nervously at Sergeant Angus. 'They're very American,' she said, feeling somehow that she must explain them. They sounded like a couple of hoodlums, but they were so *real*, somehow. They made the policeman's dignity seem even more impressive and aweful than before.

As the brake, with the police car following and the

two boys shouting beside it, approached the gate of the croft, Nicholas came from the cottage.

He was so white, Nan hardly recognized him. But she had a quick vision of how they had returned early and found the garage doors standing wide, the car missing ...

She scrambled out of the car almost before it had stopped. She ran up to Nicholas, calling as she went:

'I'm sorry! I'm sorry!'

He just stared at her. He was speechless. She had had no idea that a boy of his age could look so angry.

'Nicky. I didn't think you'd be back this early.'

He ignored her. He contrived to speak to the sergeant.

'Good afternoon,' he said, sounding, Nan thought, like a rather old clergyman.

At that moment, Charlotte came running out with Lucy at her heels.

'Oh, Angus!' cried Charlotte. 'We haven't seen you once this summer. How's Jessie?'

But Angus said rebukingly that he was on official business. 'We will speak of Jessie later.' He pulled out his notebook and slid the pencil from its place. 'It might be more seemly if we went indoors, Miss Charlotte. It is my duty to take a few particulars.'

The policemen stayed about fifteen minutes. Sergeant Angus asked a great many questions – all quite stupid and pointless, Nan decided – then he closed his notebook, rose to his feet, picked up his cap and said good afternoon. Nicholas saw the two men to the gate. Nan sat where she was, leaning her head on her hands and listening hopefully. Surely as they went away they would laugh? Or shout good-bye or something a bit lively? But they did no such thing. This was the majesty of the law in action and it was no good Nan imagining she could change it.

On the window seat, Charlotte and Lucy were sitting side by side. The two boys had been outside all the time, walking round and round the police car, poking their noses through the open window and comparing it unfavourably, in loud voices, with American police cars. But as the sergeant and his attendant constable went from the cottage and got into the car, even Alan and Roderick were silent.

Lucy said at last in an awed whisper: 'What'll happen? What'll they do to her?'

'I don't suppose we'll hear another word about it,' Charlotte replied.

'You don't? Really?' Nan said eagerly.

'It isn't as though you knocked anyone down, or anything like that. He might come back and give you a terrific talking-to, but I don't suppose it'll be anything worse ... Do cheer up, Nan. I don't wonder you did it. It must be awful having a car of your own at home – and not being allowed to drive here at all.'

'It was a crazy thing to do.'

'Well, perhaps they'll fine you,' Charlotte suggested, since Nan seemed to feel she really needed punishing.

'I didn't just do it to show off. I had your red shirt all mussed up and I just had to have another length of the red material to make it come out.'

Before Charlotte could reply, Nicholas came back into the room, with Alan and Roderick trailing uneasily behind him.

Charlotte saw at once that Nicholas was not going to be lightly parted from his anger. Perhaps, seeing that, she should have let him get it over in his own way. But Charlotte was full of warmth for Nan and knew that she was on her side. She had done a stupid thing. So what? She had done it with the best intentions and Charlotte felt she would never forgive Nicholas if he was pompous about it.

'Don't look so glum, Nicky. Wasn't Angus marvellous? I've never seen him being a proper policeman before. I think he's terribly good at it.'

'There's been no need for you to see him being a policeman,' Nicholas replied in a cold, bitter voice. 'This family's always behaved with common sense. Whenever Angus has been to this house it's been about *comfortable* things – like collecting money for the orphanage, or bringing Sarah some of Jessie's marmalade. He's been a *friend.*'

'He's still the friendliest cop *I* ever saw,' said Roderick.

'Oh shut up!' snapped Nicholas. 'I'm sick of the sound of your voice. You and Alan – you've been at it all day – yap yap – I could hear you half-way across the loch. I don't wonder Murdo brought us in early.'

'*That* was because he thought the wind was getting up,' Lucy broke in indignantly.

'Anyway,' Charlotte said quickly, 'you're being a bit unreasonable, aren't you? I've heard you complain you couldn't get a word out of the boys – you said they only talked to one another.'

'I'm still complaining about that – I just wish they wouldn't do it at the tops of their voices. What's more, I'm sick of their silly Yankee slang!'

'Oh Nicky – for heaven's sake . . .'

'And whose side are you on?' he demanded.

'I'm not on anybody's *side*. I thought we'd given up sides, anyway. I thought – I thought –'

'You thought we were just one big happy family, I suppose?'

'All right – if you like. I don't care if it sounds corny – that *is* what I thought. What I hoped, anyway.'

'You're so simple and optimistic, my dear, it just isn't true.'

'Look,' Nan said. 'This is all my fault. I did a stupid thing. I know it was a stupid thing and I'm sorry. I apologize. Won't that do? Do you have to go bawling out your own sister?'

'Don't you understand what you've done?' Nicholas cried, ignoring this. 'You've turned a friend into an enemy!'

Charlotte laughed. Really, he was too absurd – it was impossible to be angry with him. Angus was no more an enemy than Murdo, and never would be. She could not let Nicholas get away with these high dramatics. The laugh burst from her. But the instant it did so she saw that she had made a dreadful mistake.

Nicholas knew he was making a fool of himself but he could not stop. He had gone too far. It was not only that he was ridding himself of every grievance, large or small, real or imaginary, that had piled up inside him ever since he had learnt from his mother that Robert Graham had a family of four. It was much more than that. Like Charlotte, he was bitterly disappointed that they had started quarrelling again. He, too, had felt easy and relaxed because at last they seemed to have found common ground. Quite apart from missing his mother, who had always made the summer holidays so immensely successful, he found that the longer Robert was away the more he wanted him to return. It had seemed to Nicholas that they were on the verge of sending to Sarah and Robert and imploring them to return – assuring them that it would be all right now – that they had found their level together and all was well.

Almost worst of all for Nicholas was the fact that he knew that he was the one who was breaking down all this great promise. He had allowed his temper to get the better of him from the moment he discovered Nan had taken the car – largely, as he well knew, because he was jealous of her ability. After that, all the old grievances had come crowding back. He could not, for his dignity's sake, escape from his fury now. He felt as though he was on some kind of helter skelter, sliding down and round, down and round, with every twist gathering speed.

'How splendid that you're amused, my dear girl,' he said, falling on play acting. 'There's nothing I like better than loyalty. Here I am, defending the family honour, and all you can do is laugh in my face. Very pretty.'

'Stop it, Nicholas,' Charlotte said, quite quietly.

Lucy suddenly flung herself at Charlotte, clasping her round the waist and crying: 'Why can't he go away some place? He's being *awful*! Oh I think I'll go throw myself in the lake!'

'Make it the loch,' said Nicholas.

Nan sprang to her feet, slapping both hands hard down on the table.

'I've had enough! I've said I'm sorry for what happened – haven't I said I'm sorry? I have, too – and I don't mind saying it again. You may not think this is one big happy family, Nicholas Latymer, and I never did see anything less happy right now. But you're the odd man out – no one else of us. It's you who doesn't belong. And I don't care one little bit who hears me say so.'

Charlotte sat hard on her hands, for she would gladly have struck Nan for saying that. But just then, Nan was right and Charlotte knew it. They were all ranged against him.

He stood looking round at them as though he hated them. To find Nan against him, the two boys – that was nothing new. But Charlotte ... And Lucy ...

'Okay,' he said, sneering. 'If I may coin a phrase – okay, okay!'

Then he turned and went out of the room, slamming the door so hard that the china rattled on the dresser.

It was Alan who broke the silence.

'Oh-oh – what wouldn't I give right now for a sight of Winterfield, Mass.'

'Me, too,' said Roderick. 'Yes, sir – me, too. Don't you wish you were back home, Lucy?'

'No, I don't!' cried Lucy. 'I just wish I was right back before I was born!'

Nicholas spent the evening in his room, whistling a lot. The rest gradually thawed out, and although they failed to become particularly cheerful, they did not squabble among themselves – which would certainly have happened a short while ago. When supper was cooked and ready, Charlotte and Nan looked a question at one another, and Charlotte said: 'I'll go – ' and ran upstairs and knocked on her brother's door.

'What?' he called without opening.

'Supper.'

'Thanks very much – I'm skipping supper.'

'Oh come on – trout – your own catch.'

'Sorry. Not in the mood.'

Charlotte stood outside the door, wondering if she should try again. But she was afraid of making matters worse, so she went away sadly.

The fish was not as good as last time – it had stuck to

the pan and broken. At one point in the meal Charlotte found herself suddenly unable to swallow. When supper was over she left the rest to do the washing-up and went to find Alison.

The sky was clear now, but yellowish still in the extreme west, though the sun had been down a long time. The strong wind was blowing out of a cloudless expanse, and there was no further sign of the storm Murdo kept promising them. That afternoon, when they were out in the middle of the loch, the sudden springing of the strong wind had caused Murdo to turn early for home. It was a great pity that he had been so cautious.

Alison was in the kitchen making jam.

'The MacPhersons had a load of damsons off the afternoon ferry. There'll be a pound or two over for you, but I'm powerful short of jars.'

'We've got some, I think.'

'Well,' said Alison, stirring the purplish bubbling brew, 'I see you had a call from Angus Macdonald.'

'It was about the car.'

'Murdo said it was likely that, or I'd have been over to see did you need any help.'

'We did need help, Alison. There was an awful row when he'd gone. Nicky behaved like a lunatic, and I was fed up with him, and now we're all at sixes and sevens again.' As she said it, she knew it was not sixes and sevens at all, but five and one. She had never before been separated in this way from Nicholas.

'Dearie, dearie,' said Alison, shaking her head. 'You know what your Auntie Mag would have said – One step forward and two steps back . . .'

'What's so awful is that Sarah and – and the Laird'll

be back soon – and they'll find us still at it. Still fighting.'

'What's that you've taken to calling Mr Graham? The Laird, is it?'

Charlotte blushed. 'Don't laugh. I know it sounds a bit silly. But it's a sort of nickname we found for him.'

'Very good, very good,' said Alison soothingly. 'Does he know?'

'Not yet. And I shouldn't think we'll ever be able to tell him.'

'Why's that?'

'Who'd want to be Laird over a lot of quarrelsome good-for-nothings?'

'There now, there's a state of mind to be in! Have you not heard tell how there's quarrelling within a clan? It is because they are not all members of one family at all, but only families of one clan. But the laird's the laird, whatever.'

Alison bent over the pan as she spoke, skimming and testing for a set, and never looking once to right or left. In the silence that grew strangely between them then, Charlotte watched the firm sensible face and felt some of her heaviness magically leaving her.

'Alison –'

'What is it now, my lass?'

'I think you've given me something to think about.'

'Maybe,' said Alison. 'Will you run, now, and fetch those jars you have at home. The set's just right.'

11 | Murdo's Storm

When Lucy woke next morning she remembered at
once how she had wished she had never been born. The
sun was at the window, the blue curtains with the
pattern of flying gulls were blown out in the strong
blustering wind. Lucy changed her mind about wishing
she had never been born, but she still felt it would be a
long time before she would want to speak to any single
member of that household. She knew what Alan and
Roderick meant about wanting to go home, and yet she
was far from feeling homesick. She felt other things,
but not that. She had a curious unease like a weight
inside her, but she did not know what to call it.

She lay quite still in her bed. On the wall opposite was a little painting of Sarah's showing Kilmorah in winter, with snow along the edge of the sea. Lucy felt she would like to know more about the painting. She would like Sarah to tell her. But Sarah was far away.

She listened to discover whether Nan in the other bed was awake or sleeping. She was awake. She was lying there watching the curtain just as Lucy had done. Lucy sat up in bed, and Nan said without turning her head:

'It looks like the sky's full of gulls. Did you know Charlotte had Alison sew those new curtains just for us? Did you know this was really Charlotte's room, and she had them move another bed in?'

Lucy did not reply. She got up and dressed and went downstairs, all without a word. No one was about. The MacBogus was sitting crookedly on a chair in the kitchen. Outside, the boys still slept in their tent, which flapped like a sail in the stiff wind.

The morning was full of glitter and glory. Lucy saw Geordie come out of his door and run with a dish to the chicken house. She watched him let out the birds and throw down the meal for them. For a moment he stood there, a white froth to his knees as the hens fluttered and squawked and jumped and pecked in their excitement.

'Geordie!' called Lucy. She was glad to find she still had a voice inside her. She ran to the gate of the croft. 'You're out of your bed early, Geordie Monroe.'

He grinned and opened his mouth – was he really going to speak? But he closed it again, obviously deciding that the emergency was not great enough for him to make the effort. And indeed at that moment his mother appeared in the doorway and, as usual, did his talking for him.

'It's the school outing the day, Lucy. Will you not be going? They've no less than four places left in the bus, Mrs Macdonald was saying. Geordie'd like fine for you to go along.'

Geordie gave his wide toothless grin and shifted his feet about.

'There!' cried his mother in triumph. 'He's as pleased as I said.'

'What time?' Lucy asked. 'How much? Where to?'

'Ask at the post office how much. There's a picnic tea at Glenfinnan, that I know.'

'Glenfinnan! That's where Bonny Prince Charlie summoned the clans to meet him. That's where he raised his standard. Isn't it, Mrs Monroe?'

'Aye, there was something,' she agreed. 'I'm a Lowlander mysel' but I've heard it told. The bus leaves at nine-thirty, so you'd best not be dallying.'

'Okay, Geordie. I'll come. See you at half after nine.'

Lucy did not mention the school outing at breakfast. If the meal had been a cheerful one, then she would have done so. But it was dreary. Though Nicholas had reappeared, when he spoke he did so in a politely icy voice that froze Lucy's spine. Charlotte and Nan spoke to one another in normal voices, and included Lucy in their conversation as far as it was possible to include anyone who seemed unwilling to talk. Being accustomed to Geordie, Lucy knew exactly how they must feel. Outside, the two boys talked together in irritating whispers.

As soon as the meal was over, Lucy went upstairs, collected her money, retied her hair, picked up her blue windcheater and left the house without a word to a soul.

'They'll worry,' she told Geordie, as they set out together. 'As if I care.'

When they reached the post office Lucy stamped inside and asked Mrs Macdonald if there was still a place on the bus.

'There's two still. Though you're not a pupil at the school, you'll be welcome. Tell Miss MacDougal – for I've no tickets. Miss MacDougal and Miss Ross are in charge.'

At nine-thirty, Lucy climbed into the bus with the rest of a gabbling crowd, grabbed a place by the window, which meant Geordie had to sit on the gangway side with a very poor view, and was driven away shouting with all the rest on the annual outing of Kilmorah School, first to places as yet unnamed, and finally to Glenfinnan at the head of Loch Shiel.

That morning, Charlotte and Nan made up the picnic lunch together, not talking much and not expecting much enjoyment from the day. Nicholas had already gone off on his own, and the other boys were nowhere to be seen. Lucy was presumably somewhere with Geordie. In due course, the two girls collected together the usual paraphernalia of rugs and baskets and towels and walked off slowly towards the shore.

The shortest way to their usual camping place was over the top of the highest dune, and that was the way they chose now. It was not until they reached the top that they realized what a wind was blowing. It hit them as their heads emerged from the shelter of the dune. The sand was being lifted and whipped into whirls. It blew into their eyes and mouths, so that they cried out

160

and plunged swiftly down to the shore as though in this way they would escape the wind.

But they saw immediately they could open their eyes that the fair outlook to which they had become accustomed had completely changed. The sun had slid behind strands of cloud, not white nor grey, but touched with yellow. The blue had almost gone out of the sea, leaving it merely dirty and flecked with sudden fierce spurts of spray as the wind broke the swell.

'It's Murdo's storm,' said Charlotte.

'It looks grim. I wouldn't like to go in that ocean.'

'Where are the two boys?' Charlotte asked.

'The two boys' always meant Alan and Roderick, not any other combination of the three boys in the family. As she looked along the beach, anxiety flicked at Charlotte's too vivid imagination. She seemed to see the pair tossed in a sea suddenly boiling up into real tumult. And as she allowed this gruesome thought to enter her mind, she realized that the shore was utterly deserted. There were no visitors come by car to spend the day on the sands. There were no parked cars, no children digging, nothing and no one in all the wide shallow curve to south and west of the headland.

'It's kind of eerie,' Nan said. She frowned at Charlotte. 'Don't look that way, honey – you scare me. You don't have second sight or anything awful, do you?'

'Where do you think they can be?' Charlotte insisted.

'I guess they're around some place. You're usually glad when they go off on their own.'

Charlotte pulled a face. It was true that, like Nicholas, she found Alan and Roderick a trial. She must have become accustomed to them without knowing it. Her uneasiness grew in her. It was all very well for Nan to say she looked as though she had second sight – just at that moment she almost felt she had. The certainty of a coming storm filled her with strange and quite unfamiliar fears.

'And where's Lucy, for that matter?'

'She'll be with Geordie. Come on, Charlotte. What'll we do? Get on back home and batten down hatches?'

She was laughing and Charlotte did her best to laugh, too.

'Not till the crew's aboard, Nan.'

At that moment the two boys came running along the shore, heads down into the wind.

'What's *happening*?' cried Alan. 'It looks like the end of the world.'

'It's Murdo's storm,' Charlotte said again. 'You know he's been talking about it for days.'

Roderick moved close to Nan, surprisingly hanging on to her arm.

'It wouldn't be a hurricane would it?'

'We have hurricanes at home,' Nan explained. 'They scare the living daylights out of us.'

'How'd you like it if the roof blew off, Charlotte?' Alan demanded.

'We don't get hurricanes here, Alan. Still, we do get terrific storms – though it's early in the year for a really bad one. Come on – let's get home. It's silly to stay here. If it rains, it'll simply bucket down.'

As they neared home, Nicholas met them. He seemed to have forgotten about the quarrel – or else he was glad of an excuse – for he called out at once:

'I was just coming to find you. There's a perfectly frightful weather forecast – Euan just came back from the village and told me. Gales all along the coast – terrific force. They're pulling the boats up and lashing down tarpaulins. It's grim, he says.'

'Heavens! Have we got any tarpaulins we ought to lash?'

'Well, we'd better get the tent down.'

'Where'll we sleep?' cried Roderick.

'You can have the Laird's room for tonight,' Charlotte told him. 'Nicky – do you know where Lucy is?'

'Yes I do – and that's not the least of it,' Nicholas replied. 'Euan says she went off with Geordie on the school outing. They're not due back before half past six this evening. By then the storm should be just about at its height.'

During the rest of the morning and half-way into the afternoon, the wind maintained its force but showed no sign of increasing. But at four o'clock the light began to go. The sky piled up great heaps of torn cloud that began to shift and boil over the sea, lying heavily across the waves and blotting out the horizon.

Alison came running across from her own cottage with a scarf tied over her head. When she got inside she had to wait a moment to get her breath back.

'Are you all right here? Are you snug? I doubt I'll be able to get from under my own roof in an hour's time. I wanted to be sure you have everything you need.'

'I think we have. It sounds like a siege.'

'It will be. Oh that Lucy! What a day to go gallivanting off with never a word!'

'The bus comes home to the post office, doesn't it?' Nicholas asked. 'I'll go down and meet her when the time comes.'

'You bide where you are and let Murdo go. It'll likely be pouring cats and dogs by then and he has the car.'

It was an unfortunate reminder, but it passed. There was no point in personal squabbles now when the increasing storm gave them all a feeling of urgency and of banding together against a common danger. When Alison had gone, Charlotte suggested playing cards.

With the lamps lit already, they settled down round the table. The wind beat furiously at the window, but the cottage, firm as a rock with its two-foot-thick walls, seemed merely to settle itself farther into the earth. It took the wind on its shoulders and was unshaken.

Just before six they peered from the windows and saw Murdo go by. He hooted and waved as he went. In the last hour the wind had increased greatly. The stunted trees at the gate were bent almost double, sand was blowing from the dunes, and the air was full, not of rain, but of salt spray blown inland. The sky was darker

with every minute. If it went on like this it would be deep night by half past six.

'The bus is sure to be delayed,' Nicholas said, as time went on and Murdo did not return. 'Shall we change to racing demon?'

The girls were sick of cards, but Nicholas and the other two boys continued. Nan fetched her sewing, cut out a new right sleeve for the red shirt and set about making good her mistake.

Charlotte could not settle to anything. She walked from window to window, fidgeted and sighed and bit her nails in impatience and anxiety. A storm so huge must be sweeping the entire country. Where was Sarah now? If they were driving along some open road, would the Laird know how to get them to shelter? That was a silly thought, but she was unable to check her imagination as it raced over every possible disaster that could befall . . .

'Here he comes!'

She had seen the car lights approaching. Everyone leapt up and rushed to the window to watch Murdo's blue car pull up at the gate.

'He's alone!'

Murdo got out of the car, hanging on to the door as he did so to prevent its being snatched out of his hand. He came up the path with his head down, bearing into the wind. Charlotte opened the door and he came straight inside.

'What's happened? Where is she?'

'They're not yet back. Mistress Macdonald had a telephone call from Sandy MacIver who is driving them. They were barely ten miles on their way, he said, and he'd be ringing again. But the lines are down out of the village now and there's no getting through.'

'The telegraph lines? Oh Murdo – that's really bad.'

'It's fierce. I cannot mind the like these thirty years.'

'What shall we do now?' Nicholas asked.

'There's nothing to do but bide quiet. If they have not returned in another hour, then some should go out and look for them. Maybe they're stranded. If there was a great tree across the road, that would prevent them passing. Two or three cars could bring the youngest home.'

An hour seemed a long time to wait. Murdo returned to the village. Charlotte tried to think about planning the supper. Nan went on sewing. Nicholas and Alan and Roderick changed from racing demon to snap and even beggar-my-neighbour.

'I think we should eat something,' Nicholas said at last. 'One of us should go in the car with Murdo, in case he needs help.'

'Help? Do you think something awful's happened?'

'No of course not, Nan. But branches come down and sometimes you need a saw before you can clear them. We must take one with us – and a hatchet. It would be crazy for one person alone – it'd take hours to get through.'

'All right, then,' Charlotte said. 'Supper now. Help me, Nan, will you?'

When they were half-way through the meal, Murdo came again to the door, and again he was alone – but this time they expected him to be.

'What's happening?'

'Mr Forbes and Miss Cameron have set out. Also Andrew MacDougal with Donald, his brother. Sandy MacIver knows the road like his own hand. At least they will not turn the wrong way.'

'There must be something we can do?'

'There is something. If I give Euan my car to drive, I think your good mother would agree I should take hers. It is bigger – we could bring back six children.'

'Yes, of course,' Nicholas agreed. 'That's far the best thing to do.'

'Then have you blankets?' Murdo asked Charlotte. 'They'll be tired and maybe frightened. It would be wise to wrap them up.'

At once Charlotte ran to the big blanket box in Sarah's room. Nan put on the kettle and got out the vacuum flasks they used for picnics. By the time Murdo had handed over to Euan and brought the brake to the door, everything was ready.

'I'll come with you,' Nicholas said, raking out his duffel coat from the cupboard under the stairs.

'Yes, come,' Murdo agreed. 'It is one less place but I may need help with fallen timber. Euan should have had a passenger – it was foolish to send him on. It is never wise to travel alone in a bad storm.' He looked at Nan. 'If you would make one of us, we will overtake Euan and have two to each car.'

Nan said quickly: 'Sure. I'll get my coat.'

'Can't we go, too?' Alan cried.

'We don't want to fill up the car with sightseers,' Nicholas said. He gave Charlotte a rather doubtful grin. 'Sorry. Orders.'

She nodded. She wanted desperately to go with him. She thought Murdo had chosen Nan so that he would have one from each family; perhaps he even thought this would be best in case there was an accident; perhaps he was insuring against losing Sarah both her children. This was not altogether Charlotte's wild imagination at work. Terrible tragedies had occurred in storms less violent than this one.

When Nan came downstairs she had changed into slacks and a windcheater and tied a scarf over her head. Because she was a slim, rather fragile creature, this made her look gallant and determined. Charlotte would have been ready to hug her and kiss her good-bye, only it seemed a bit silly. So she just said: 'Mind how you go,' in a casual voice, as though they were going out to post letters. Under her breath she added: *'Kilmorah to the end of time.'*

Nicholas flicked Charlotte a look but said nothing.

'Come on, Nicole Ann,' he said. 'Take a deep breath.'

Charlotte stood holding the door and peering after them. Soon the car was moving off. She closed the door with difficulty. She had the feeling that the storm was trying to force its way inside. Without thinking, instinctively, she bolted the door.

Alan said: 'You told us you don't have hurricanes in Scotland. But it is a hurricane – it is! What'll happen if the roof blows off?'

'It won't,' replied Charlotte cheerfully.

'If a tree blew down,' said Roderick, 'would it kill them? If it fell on the car?'

'Where d'you figure Daddy is now? Could a tree fall on him?'

'You're a fine pair!' Charlotte cried. 'Stop it! Come on – let's finish up the supper. Now the others have gone, we can have two helpings each.'

They sat round the table, stolidly working their way through apple pie and loathing it.

'Have you ever had a holiday – a vacation – on your own before?' Charlotte asked, for the sake of making conversation.

'Once. We had a cabin in the mountains. We were

there a week, then Daddy came too. But we had neighbours there. They looked after us.'

'Well, we've got Alison and Murdo and Euan,' Charlotte said.

'We've got Alison,' replied Roderick, darkly. 'We haven't got Murdo or Euan right now.'

'Never mind about that. Come on – help me with the washing up. We'll just have to leave the pie.'

As they turned together from the table, she found herself between the two of them. Poor little boys, she thought, full of softness and warmth. She put an arm round each, feeling how their skinny shoulders hunched with fear and misery. She knew how they felt. As though the whole world was empty of everything but storm and danger. As if there was no one else living but the three of them.

That was how she felt, too.

12 | The Clan

Although Murdo had said the telegraph lines were down, even Nicholas, who had seen storms before in these parts, was not prepared for the havoc. Wires were all over the road, poles leaning insanely or else actually fallen. Once out of doors it was not dark, but livid with the light of storm. Twigs, branches, leaves whirled through the air. Hay ricks were torn apart and great swathes of hay caught on wires and bushes. As they came out along the lochside and the road began to rise, they could see the entire surface of the Sound, and farther east the loch, whipped up into spray that was so blown it looked as if an unending wave swept inwards from the sea. And this spray blew farther, filling the air, burning green leaves brown and withering where it touched.

As soon as they were among trees the noise of the wind was terrific. It snatched at the car, buffeted it and beat it until it seemed the very sides must be dented. A film of salt soon covered the windscreen, even though their backs were now to the sea, and the wipers could only clear them a fan-shaped space to peer through. Ahead of them as they drove they saw tail lights that must be Euan's. Then these put on speed and vanished. Murdo at the wheel, Nan and Nicholas beside him, were as isolated at that moment as Charlotte and the boys left at home. They had, however, the satisfaction of being up and doing.

There was a radio in the car and after a bit Nicholas switched it on. Somehow they expected it to have news for them, they almost thought it would guide them and reassure them, or warn them of dangers ahead. But there was only a programme of light gay music, so broken by the surge and splutter of atmospherics that Nicholas switched off again.

'I believe the weather's getting worse, MacMurdo. The trees sound horrific.'

'Not a doubt but many will fall,' Murdo agreed.

And indeed they were creaking and wailing and splintering.

'Oh look – look!' Nan cried.

As the car took a slight turn by the gate of a large house standing back at the end of a driveway, the sweep of the headlights showed them an enormous spruce leaning before the wind, shrieking in all its great strength as it fell, not snapping, but dragging the root right out and with it a huge clot of earth yards across.

It was a relief to come out from under the trees and move on to a stretch of open road. Yet here the force of the wind was such that it threatened the car. The wild air was full of tumult and strange cries, like a storm in Shakespeare or perhaps in some old story of heroes and Vikings.

'What's that ahead?' Nicholas said suddenly.

A car was pulled off the road, the bonnet was open and two angry men, the MacDougals, were trying to get it going again.

'What is it?' Murdo shouted.

'It is the pump! The pump!' came the furious reply. 'It is the petrol pump has deserted on us! We have spoken to Euan and he will try for help at Inverloch.'

Murdo could only drive on, leaving the angry pair behind. Now they travelled in silence, aware that any car in the world can suddenly pack up and refuse to stir – and what if it should happen to theirs?

'That'll be Euan again,' Murdo said suddenly.

The red lights of a car ahead seemed like the face of a friend. Then they saw that they did not move. Soon they could see in their own headlights that a tree had fallen. Either it had crashed on the car or the car had crashed into it.

Murdo braked and stopped. 'Wait here.' He was out of the car at speed, pausing only to be certain the door was latched and could not be torn off.

'Nicky – what's happened?'

'Almost anything, I should think.'

'You mean – he could be killed?'

'What d'you think yourself?'

Nan did not answer. Nicholas could feel her shivering as she sat beside him.

They watched Murdo fight his way through the wind as a man fights his way through water to the thigh. They saw him reach the car and peer in. The headlights showed them this picture at the end of a beam, like a picture thrown on to a screen. Then they saw him look back and beckon with a wide sweeping movement.

'You stay here, Nan.' Nicholas got out of the car carefully. 'Keep the headlights up.'

He collected the saw and the hatchet and battled his way towards Murdo. The force of the wind pressed upon him and almost stopped his breath. It was like being squeezed in a giant's hand.

'What's happened?' The words were pumped out of Nicholas, he gasped like a fish. 'Is Euan hurt?'

'Not too much. But he's a nasty bang on the head.'

This was a considerable understatement. Euan looked ghastly. He had tried to brake to avoid the tree, and in doing so had flung himself against the dashboard. He had cut the right side of his face from the temple downwards and he was bleeding badly. He looked more green than white in the unreal light of the storm and the headlights from the car behind. None the less he grinned when he saw Nicholas peering in at him.

'Saturday is never like to be a good day for me,' he said.

They had to decide what to do. The car and the fallen tree were blocking the road and Euan was in no fit state to help clear it. To clear it, however, was the obvious first step, and Murdo and Nicholas set about the job.

'To think there's two strong men at the roadside not three miles gone,' Murdo said, almost groaning.

Nan came running when she saw what was happening.

'That's bad,' she said, inspecting Euan's head. 'Do you have a first-aid kit? Is it in the trunk?'

'Boot,' said Nicholas, unable to resist the correction, even though he was struggling to tug a large branch clear of the road.

When it was mopped up the cut looked better, but it needed stitching. However much he denied it, Euan was badly shocked. His teeth chattered and his hands shook, to his extreme fury. He could not possibly drive on. Nor could he be left there alone.

'You need a doctor, laddie,' Murdo said, when he and Nicholas had hauled the tree free of the rather battered car. 'Let me think how. I'm unwilling to leave the car by the roadside – with this wind and the drop down through the trees I doubt we'd see her again.' He frowned and was silent. 'I have taken a decision,' he said at last. 'I shall drive Euan to the doctor at Inverloch.'

'But we can't just stay here, MacMurdo,' Nicholas cried. 'What about the wind and the drop through the trees for us? We'll have to get on somehow. We came out to look for the bus and we haven't found it yet.'

'Did I say you should wait? It is reasonable to suppose there will be others setting out to help, the longer the bus is away. But they may be stopped a dozen times before they reach you. And we have no knowledge of what has become of Mr Forbes and Miss Cameron. They may be far ahead or they may be stopped just as Euan has been. No. It is necessary that you should go on. I'll be clapped in Glasgow Jail, not a doubt of it. But I'm telling you, Miss Nan, to drive the brake as you well know how. And good luck to you.'

'Sure,' said Nan very calmly. 'I'll drive on behind you, Murdo, just as soon as you get on your way.'

She turned and went back to the car, fighting the wind still, and Nicholas followed her.

'It's started to rain. Are you all right, Nan?'

'Aren't you?'

He grinned. 'My life is in your hands.'

'Come on, then – let's go.'

They followed Murdo, as indeed they had no choice. The rain was now pouring down, washing off the salt spray but running so freely down the windscreen that the wipers were not able to keep the glass clear.

'It'll be worse when we turn for home,' Nicholas said.

'Right now I feel we never shall!'

When they reached Inverloch, Murdo pulled up and Nan tucked in behind him. Murdo got out and came back to them. As he stood at the window the rain poured down his face and beat in on Nan listening to him. In spite of the rain, a jagged hole had appeared in the clouds and the moon gave faint snatches of light. The ground was littered with broken branches and on the slopes bordering the road six and seven trees at a time were down and tumbled one on another.

'Euan is worse than I feared,' Murdo said. 'Should it happen the doctor is already out, as he may well be, I must drive on to the hospital at Fort William. I fear they are in some trouble with the bus. We are now a long way from home.'

'Suppose we don't find it?' Nicholas asked.

'You must turn back and leave it to others. It is possible Sandy MacIver has chosen to drive to shelter at Fort William and they may get a message back. Use your good sense, both of you, and do not run into danger needlessly. I trust you.'

As he spoke, headlights appeared moving in the oncoming direction. A Land-Rover appeared and pulled up beside them. It carried one of the maintenance gangs from the council, out to keep the roads clear, if that were possible.

'Did you see the bus from Kilmorah?' Murdo shouted to the foreman.

'Never a sign. You're the second to ask.'

'Then the first would be Mr Forbes and Miss Cameron,' Murdo said. 'Did they drive on?'

'They did. But I doubt they'll get through. The road's

blocked time and again. The heavy trucks are on their way with chains and electric saws.'

'I've an injured man to get to the doctor,' Murdo said.

'Then you're in luck. Dr Lang has just driven into the village ahead of us. He's likely in his parlour yet. It's as well, for you could not get him by telephone now. The lines are down from Fort William to the coast.'

Then the Land-Rover squeezed by them, here where the road was a shade wider as it came into the village, and roared away.

Murdo looked at Nicholas and Nan.

'I hope fine I've done the right thing to bring you. Be sensible and have a care now, do.'

'Get Euan to the doctor,' Nan shouted at him. 'See you!'

Then in her turn she passed Murdo and sped away confidently on the continuing search.

Once they were on their own, Nicholas and Nan were filled with a renewed sense of urgency. For all Murdo's talk of Sandy MacIver running for shelter to the town, they knew that what they might find could be a disaster. This feeling was intensified by the words of the foreman shouting through the gale -- *The lines are down from Fort William to the coast.* It was the sort of thing they might expect to hear in a play or a film – the words would have made them bunch up tightly as they sat in the dark watching some imaginary adventure played out. But this was real. This was Nicholas Latymer and Nan Graham driving through darkness and storm towards what might turn out to be a scene of disaster, of tragedy. For the first time they knew that tales they had read of accident and death could happen, too, to them. They were plunged into the kind of situation which could make headlines – this time they would not be headlines about strangers.

'I thought it was getting quieter,' Nicholas said. 'But if you ask me it's blowing harder than ever.'

He peered through the streaming windscreen, which was plastered suddenly with blown leaves whipped against the glass.

'Are we still on the road, would you say?'

'I'd say – just about. Gosh – it's terrific. The trees!
The trees! Nan! Nan – look out!!!'

As he shouted a tree ahead of them was already falling. Slowly, slowly it bent across the road. Time stood
still as they tried to calculate the instants until it would
be so far angled that it could only crash down across the
roadway.

Nan had time to count – and yet no time for anything but a split-second decision. In the darkness it was
almost impossible to gauge the distance between the
nose of the car and the falling tree. She resisted the
impulse to brake hard – not only because she knew that
she might brake too soon, that she might stop the car
on the very spot where the tree must fall, but aware too
that if they were this side of it they might have to stay
there.

Almost without knowing what she was doing, she
stepped hard on the throttle pedal. The car bounded
forward like a horse at a gate. As it leapt over the
ground, the branches of the falling tree struck its rear.
The car rocked and faltered. Nan kept her foot down.
Then the branches slithered off the back and the tree
crashed on the roadway.

There was a bend ahead. As she heard the tree hit the
ground behind her, Nan swung the wheel with a sensation of high excitement, knowing that she had done the
right thing, knowing that she had taken a terrible
chance and won through. As the wind picked itself up
once more and beat over the loch face a hundred feet
below, Nan shouted to Nicholas:

'Honey – are you still there?'

'Just. You?'

'Oh sure – I'm here all right. Did you feel how she

jumped for me? Did you? She's a wonderful little old automobile! She's a wonder!'

'Tell you what,' said Nicholas. 'I'll be able to get a driving licence in November – and so will you. How about you give me lessons, sister?'

'*Okay!*' cried Nan. 'It's a date!'

Then they both cried out: 'November?'

'Well, then – Christmas, Nan.'

'But where'll we be?'

There seemed little doubt that they might be apart. What was to happen, anyway, once this summer was over? Perhaps they had all, at one time or another, had some idea of alternating between England and America. But could they expect to be for ever flying the Atlantic? Suddenly it was so obvious that they were going to want to.

Nicholas said, quiet angrily: 'Something'll have to be arranged, that's all.'

'Oh I'm sure it will be. I'm sure!'

'It'll have to be. It'll just have to be. Well – hell! – I've got to have my driving lessons, haven't I?'

Nan began to chuckle.

'Now what's the matter?'

'I was just thinking – poor Daddy! Six children's an awful lot to please!' She suddenly braked and the car slithered a bit on the streaming wet road. 'Look! Isn't that a light?'

'Where? Yes – I believe there is something. But it's below the road. Must be a cottage...'

'I don't think so...' She stopped the car now and switched off the engine. 'Listen! Do you hear anything?'

They sat there, straining their ears through the

tumult of wind and rain and the beating of loch water on the shore below.

'It's singing . . .'

Nicholas half wondered if it might not be the singing of sirens risen up out of the loch as they did in the old legends.

'Oh, will you listen to that, Nicky! It's the bus. They're singing *The Twelve Days of Christmas* . . . What do you know?'

'Seems an odd time of year . . .'

'It means Lucy's there – safe.'

'I don't know how you make that out.'

'Why – that's an old American folk tune.'

'It's *what*? Nan! It's as English as steak-and-kidney pudding . . .'

But she was already running towards the light and he had to follow. He would have to put her right about that another time. Now, it was enough to grope towards the singing and the light to where the bus slanted with its nose in the soft side of the bank. It would never get out of there without a crane.

Nicholas shouted: 'Miss MacDougal! Sandy!'

Nan shouted: 'Lucy! Geordie!'

The singing stopped abruptly. Instantly a crowd of children struggled towards the door up the bus's sloping floor, and Miss MacDougal put her head out of the window.

'Are you the rescue team?'

The pair looked at the bus, at the milling children, some laughing, some shouting indignantly that they wanted to go home, some half crying. It was a tall order, they felt, that they were asked to fill.

'We just came to look for you.'

'And you've found us,' said Miss MacDougal. 'Not a

moment too soon. Sandy's gone looking for help. He fixed the lights before he went, but the battery's looking a bit sick. I wouldn't fancy being here much longer in the dark.'

Under Miss MacDougal's elbow as she hung on to the window, Lucy suddenly appeared.

'Oh Nicky – you said not to want rescuing three times. Will you look what's happened?'

'Are you all right, Lucy honey . . .?'

'Oh sure I'm all right. Why wouldn't I be?' But as she spoke, Lucy's angry voice wavered into a wail. 'Can't you get Sarah back, Nan? Aren't we friends enough yet? I guess we need looking after a little . . .'

Before Nan could make any reply to that challenge, headlights swept along the road from either direction – Sandy with a heavy breakdown lorry on one side, Sergeant Angus and his young constable on the other, with behind them Mr Forbes and Miss Cameron, who had somehow missed the way in all the chaos and confusion and were now retracing their steps.

'Oh – oh,' said Nan, spotting Angus.

'Is it yourself, Miss Graham?' called the sergeant. 'I have Murdo with me. He has left Euan at the hospital and he'll be glad to drive you home. It's a lucky chance when you have the right person to call on in an emergency.'

Did he mean she was lucky to have Murdo to call on, or that Murdo had been lucky to have her? Nan would probably never know.

In pouring, bitter rain, but with the wind abating a little, the children were transferred in ones and twos from the bus to the various cars – and more were arriving as those friends and relations who had set out from Kilmorah after Murdo and the others had left, came through one by one, the blocks on the road having been cleared by the gangs.

'It is eleven o'clock!' cried a boy's voice. 'That is a wonderful thing for me to be out at eleven o'clock!'

It sounded almost like Geordie.

Neither Nan nor Nicholas would have been surprised if he had said it was four in the morning. They seemed to have been on the road since the day before yesterday. And they were not home yet.

It was nearly two when Alison came across to see how Charlotte and the boys were managing. The boys were in bed, but Charlotte was huddled by the fire looking pale and wretched.

'The wind's dropping,' Alison said. 'The storm's going over now. Oh my dearie, what a poor wee thing you're looking!'

'Shall we ever see them again?' Charlotte asked.

'Will you listen to that? Have you never seen a storm before? You know what becomes of the roads hereabouts. They'll likely not get back till daybreak.'

Charlotte smiled a bit.

'I'm glad you've come. Two o'clock is a very despairing sort of time.' She looked searchingly at Alison. 'And do you think *they're* all right, too? I mean Mummy – and the Laird?'

'As right as rain – if that's not a poor way to put it.' Alison sat down by Charlotte and put her arm round her in a very comfortable way. 'Could you not tell them soon that it's time to come back?'

'Sometimes I wonder if they want to come back. I wouldn't blame them if they didn't. We're a poor lot.'

Alison smiled at that. 'Listen now,' she said, 'and mind you keep this to yourself. I've done as I was told to do and written them every other day to tell them how you were doing.'

'As you were *told* to do . . .?'

'Haven't I said so? I was half minded to tell them yon Lucy worried me – but you would keep on she was perfectly well and happy.'

'I wonder a bit –' Charlotte began. But she broke off because there was a sound outside. She sprang up. 'They're here! They're here!' She rushed to the door and flung it open as Nan and Nicholas and Lucy ran up the path. 'Oh Nicky! Oh Nan – Lucy!' And she burst into tears.

This emotional greeting upset them all a bit. Alan and Roderick came rushing downstairs in their pyjamas. They all huddled together and sniffed and then laughed – and then sniffed again. Alison left them to it, saying she had people of her own to attend to.

Charlotte had kept the fire going and kettles boiling, for all her wretchedness. She made a huge pot of tea and they all sat down on the hearthrug very close together, while the last of the storm beat on over the sturdy walls and roof of the cottage, on and on up the coast, to blow its last faint breaths out as daylight spread on the tossed sky.

'Came the dawn!' cried Nicholas.

'That's the first time I've never been to bed,' said Charlotte, not displeased. She got up from her place on the hearth and went to pull back the curtains. She stood with her back to the others because she was going to make a speech. 'Look,' she said at last, 'I had an awful lot of time to think last night. What I thought was – we ought to get Sarah and the Laird back pretty soon. Not because things have gone so awfully wrong sometimes – and not even because sometimes they've gone awfully right. But because I don't think we can do without them much longer. I don't mean we've all stopped quarrelling for ever and turned into dear little birds agreeing in their nest. I just think – well, I just think it's time they came back.' And still without looking at them, she said: 'What do you think? Shall we take a vote? Those who want them back – oh quickly, quickly – put up their hands.'

She waited. Nicholas said: 'They're up.'

Then Charlotte turned, and they were all holding up their hands and waving them – even two hands each in the case of Alan and Roderick who for once turned two into four, instead of two into one.

'Oh,' said Charlotte. 'Well. I think that's good.'

'What'll we do?' asked Nan. 'Call them up?'

'Send them a wire, Charley – shall we?'

'Yes, a wire. Let's write it now.' And Charlotte with her usual speed whipped up a notebook and a pencil and thrust them at Nicholas saying: 'You.'

Nicholas sat down with the paper and the pencil and thought hard.

'We don't need to say much, do we?'

'No. Just – *Come on home*, do you think?'

'That sounds like *Come home – all is forgiven*. Think of something else.'

'*Come back to Kilmorah . . .?*'

Nicholas nodded and wrote: '*Come back to Kilmorah*. What shall we sign it?'

'We should all sign it.'

'But that'd be such a mouthful.'

It was Charlotte's turn again, and again she was looking anywhere but at the faces of the others.

'Alison gave me an idea. She said how a clan was made up of families and sometimes the families squabbled – but it was still the clan and the laird was head . . .'

'I see what you mean,' said Nicholas, scribbling away. 'Then, how's this sound: *Come back to Kilmorah.* Signed: *The Clan.*'

Nan was the only one who managed to reply.

'Oh that's wonderful! I call that just wonderful!'

She must have been as tired as all the rest, for her voice wobbled and rocked and ended in a kind of squeak.

'But we're mad,' said Nicholas. 'I've just remembered. The lines are down from Fort William to the coast.'

'There's no way to send it.'

Faces fell. Everything had seemed wound up into a tightly-tied neat little parcel – but there was no way for the parcel to be posted.

In the growing light, one of the council Land-Rovers rattled up to the croft and stopped at the gate. The driver swung out and came up to the cottage. They had opened the door before he lifted his hand to knock. The six of them stood there, crowded together, untidy and dirty and crumpled from a night in their clothes.

'I was to bring you a message,' the man said. 'To say they were a wee bit delayed by the wild night and stopped over at Inverloch. But you're to wait breakfast for them.'

'But – but who? Do you mean . . .? Well, for goodness' sake, who gave you the message?'

'I understood it was your parents,' he replied, extremely surprised. 'Were they not expected?'

'Well,' said Charlotte. 'Yes and no.'

When he had gone they stood and looked at one another, not knowing whether they dared start laughing.

'Know what?' said Lucy. 'I think that awful Alison knew all about it all the time.'

Charlotte thought so, too. If she had been hearing every other day – and writing every other day ... A wide and cheerful smile spread over Charlotte's sleepy face.

Nicholas was looking at the message they had worked out with such care.

'What a waste.' He began sadly and reluctantly to tear the paper.

'Stop!' cried Charlotte and Nan in one breath.

'Stop?'

Charlotte looked at Nan and laughed.

'The way I figure it,' she said, 'they'll be mighty interested to see that message. What do you all think?'

About the Author

Barbara Willard went to a convent school, and then tried acting for a while. The theatre is still one of her greatest interests. Her first adult novel was published when she was twenty-two, and she went on writing about one a year until the Second World War interrupted her.

After the war she went to live in the country, working for the story departments of major film companies and as a play reader. Her first children's book, *The House with Roots*, was published by Constable in 1959, and she gave up working for film companies when she settled down to writing children's books.

She is unmarried, and likes gardening, house-painting, driving, travel, cats and dogs, and cooking, eating and drinking.

Some other Puffins you might enjoy

PONIES PLOT

C. Northcote Parkinson

The world is full of books about ponies, written for children. This is completely different, a book about children, written for ponies. Instead of the child teaching the pony how to jump – as if it didn't *know* – it is the pony who teaches the child how to ride.

From a pony's point of view, all riding schools have the same thing wrong with them: they are for children who *can't* ride. As soon as a child becomes bearable, she vanishes and has a pony of her own, and her place is taken by another. The newcomers are certain to scream when the pony walks and as likely to fall off as soon as it comes to a halt. 'Here we go again,' the ponies grumble, and who can blame them?

So under Old Smokey's tuition, the ponies each decided what sort of girl they would like, and how they were to train and discipline her when they had her.

ROLLER SKATES

Ruth Sawyer

'The last five minutes have made me an orphan,' Lucinda shouted to the hansom cab driver.

'Dear me,' said Mr Gilligan, 'as sad as that!'

'It isn't sad at all. I think it is going to be awfully pleasant. I'm not a permanent orphan. My mother and father are going abroad.'

Mr Gilligan, who took her home with him to eat real Irish griddle cake with currants in it, was the first of the new friends Lucinda made that year. It was the best year she had ever had, sleeping in the little folding-bed and skating everywhere on roller-skates, even to school and to church, reading whatever she liked and discovering Shakespeare's plays with Uncle Earle. She had more freedom than ever before, and without Aunt Emily's discipline she didn't feel the same rebellious and disagreeable person any longer.

RIBBON OF FIRE

Allan Campbell McLean

It was 1884 and the crofters in the small township in Skye were being bullied to the limit by the laird and the factor. They had already pulled down the laird's fine new wall which enclosed their old common land, and Lachlann Ban might inspire them to anything. No one else would have dared attack the factor or rescue a man from Portree gaol, or gathered such a great band to march on the laird, their peat torches a ribbon of fire through the hills.

But time and again the factor forestalled their most secret and deeply laid plans. The crofters had suffered everything in the past, but never a traitor in their midst. And if there was a traitor, who could it be?

SMITH

Leon Garfield

Smith, the pickpocket, was twelve years old and he lived in the mazy slums round St Paul's. One day an old gentleman came up Ludgate Hill. His pockets bulged provokingly, and in an instant Smith had emptied them – but at that moment two men in brown appeared. The taller came at the old man from the front, the other took on his back – and slid a knife into it.

A quarter of a mile off, Smith stopped running. What had he got this time? Something valuable. Something that had been worth the old gentleman's life. He fished it out. *A document*. He stood up, spat and cursed. He could not read.

But Smith hung on to his document. Hounded through London, pursued by the brown murderers, befriended by a blind magistrate, betrayed and flung wretchedly into Newgate gaol, he still hoped there might be something in it for him. And in a way there was.

If you have enjoyed reading this book and would like to know about others which we publish, why not join the Puffin Club? It costs 5s. and for this you will be sent the club magazine, Puffin Post, four times a year and a smart badge and membership card. You will also be able to enter all the competitions. You will find an application form on the next page.

APPLICATION FOR MEMBERSHIP OF
THE PUFFIN CLUB

(Write clearly in block letters)

To: THE PUFFIN CLUB SECRETARY,
PENGUIN BOOKS LTD,
HARMONDSWORTH,
MIDDLESEX

I would like to join the Puffin Club. I enclose my 5s. membership fee for one year and would be glad if you would send me my badge and copy of Puffin Post.

Surname ....

Christian name(s) ....

Full Address ....

....

....

Age .... Date of Birth ....

School (name and address) ....

....

Where I buy my Puffins ....

Signature (optional) .... Date ....

Note: We regret that at present applications for membership can be accepted only from readers resident in the U.K. or the Republic of Ireland.

Puffin Club - Price Increase

We regret to announce that from February 1970 the enrolment fee has been raised to 10s.